THE MERCY KILLINGS

Esther & Jack Enright Mystery Book Six

David Field

SAPERE
BOOKS

THE MERCY KILLINGS

Published by Sapere Books.

11 Bank Chambers, Hornsey, London, N8 7NN,
United Kingdom

saperebooks.com

ISBN: 978-1-912786-37-4

Chapter One

Walter Missingham pulled hard on the oars of his flat-bottomed skiff as his son Michael pushed it as far out into the floating seaweed as his long waders allowed, then jumped over its stern to join his father on their short trip out to their oyster cages. It was low tide on the Thames, and behind them lay their cottage in the village of West Mersea, on the Essex bank of the Thames Estuary. It was early April in 1896, and they could expect a decent harvest for the local market.

The water was flat and oily, and they made good progress once they were clear of the clinging seaweed that came and went with the tides. Walter rowed steadily, with the ease that came naturally to a man raised on the water from which they eked out their living, and Michael squinted into the midday sun as he watched for the first of the cages to become visible just below the surface, to alert his father when it was time to ship the oars. Upstream to his right Michael could see the bows of a coastal freighter working its way carefully down the available navigable channel on its way to Sheerness and beyond, while way out to his left in the open ocean he could just make out the funnels of a large warship under full steam ploughing its way north from Chatham.

He looked back inboard, and then past the bow of the boat, just in time to warn his father that they were nearly there. There were a dozen cages held down by hooks at this first location, and the same number a further half mile downstream; with a bit of luck they would fill all the eight mesh sacks they had brought with them, which were now lying in the scuppers awaiting their fill of fresh oysters.

The boat bumped slightly as its bow caught the front of the first row of cages that, at low tide, were barely a foot below the surface, attached to the riverbed by anchor hooks that Michael had dived to attach when he had been only fourteen. Walter grunted as he unhooked the first cage and lifted it into the boat; then they both rummaged urgently through its contents for the largest of the shells, throwing them into the open sack between the feet of their waders. The first cage yielded a promising harvest, and after replacing it on its anchor hook Walter used its top as a lever with which to pull their flat craft down to the next cage. As he did so, Michael's attention was caught by something white bobbing in the water ahead of them.

'What's that?' He nodded towards the object that had somehow got itself impaled on the metal rim of the cage furthest out into the channel. His father followed his nod and shrugged.

'Damned if I know. Let's take a look, shall we?'

Walter pushed their vessel slowly down the line of cages until he reached the final one, where a small, rounded white parcel of some sort was caught on the metal frame of the cage, just below the water line. He looked down suspiciously at it, then back up towards Michael.

'Pass me that 'ook, lad. Some'ow I doesn't like ter touch it.'

His first attempt resulted in the hook simply tearing at whatever was wrapped around the parcel and as he tried again more vigorously the bundle was dislodged from where it had been impaled and was on the point of sinking to the bottom until Walter leaned out of the boat and grabbed it with both hands, holding it high in the air as water cascaded from it. Then he swung inwards with a sudden cry of fear and disgust and dropped it into the bottom of the boat, where it landed with a dull squelch. A foul odour reached their nostrils as greeny-yellow puss oozed out from underneath it.

Walter grabbed onto his nose tightly, then leaned over the side in order to vomit copiously into the water that was lapping gently against the side of the oyster cages. Michael stared down, horror-stricken, at what his father had hauled on board, then stated the obvious.

'That don't smell too good. What is it — some sorta dead fish?'

'No, son, it ain't no fish. Push us off an' I'll row us back in.'

'What about the other cages?'

'Forget the other cages. We gotta take this in afore it stinks the boat out.'

'Can't yer just throw it back?'

His father looked back at him disbelievingly. 'Maybe yer Mam shoulda done that ter you, if that's what yer've grown up like — not carin' a damn for the dead.'

Michael wrinkled his nose. 'What *is* it?'

'It's not what it is now,' his father advised him as he prodded it enquiringly with the toe of his waders and rolled it over to face his son. 'It's what it once *were*.'

Michael turned his head sideways to get a better look at it, then all but choked as the realisation hit him.

'Bloody 'Ell! It's a bubby, innit?'

Chapter Two

Esther Enright smiled lovingly as she gazed out of the kitchen window to where five-year-old Lily was playing happily on the swing that Jack had proudly constructed on the grass strip that separated the rear steps from their vegetable patch. Beyond the neat straight mounds that revealed where he had planted seed potatoes in front of the somewhat withering survivors of last winter's cabbages was the railway line that led, to the left, into Barking Station, down Bunting Lane, along which their house — number 26 — stood out because of the fresh coat of paint that had been Jack's first job when they had moved in last Autumn.

'Mummy,' three-year-old Bertie called from the kitchen table where he sat drawing a picture of what he claimed was a horse, 'Baby Miriam's under the table.'

'She's only learning how to walk,' Esther advised him with a smile as she turned and watched their one year old stubbornly pulling herself upright with the aid of a table leg, before sitting down heavily on her padded bottom. 'She's not interfering with what you're doing, so let her do what she pleases. There was a time when you used to do that.'

Esther reflected on how much Bertie looked like the pictures she had seen of Jack as a child and marvelled at how such a spoiled and over-protected little boy had grown up into the sometimes stern, but ever just, man who was now a Detective Sergeant in the Essex Constabulary. It presumably had a lot to do with the fact that when Jack had been fourteen years old, and his father had died, his Uncle Percy had persuaded his sister-in-law to allow the boy to be brought up with him and his wife Aunt Beattie, who were childless, while Constance also had a daughter, Jack's sister Lucy, who she could bring up under her stern supervision. Percy had been — and still was — a police officer himself, and Jack had passed through his formative years idolising his uncle and adoptive father figure. When the time came to choose a career — and much to his mother's disappointed disapproval — Jack had joined the police himself.

That's how she and Jack had first met, when Esther had been a humble seamstress living in a rented room in Spitalfields, a Jewish orphan with nothing to recommend her but her dark beauty. Jack had been smitten from the outset, but his mother Constance had needed more persuading, until she came to appreciate that Esther's upbringing and education had been the best that her wealthy textile importer parents could provide for her, until their tragic deaths in a river accident had left the poor girl to fend for herself. The fact that she'd done so with modesty and pride, avoiding all the obvious pitfalls that lay in wait for a single girl in the East End of London, had impressed Constance to the point that she'd actually encouraged and supported Jack when he'd announced his intention of marrying Esther eight years ago.

Esther and Constance had inevitably had their confrontations, until her mother-in-law had finally realised that meeting Esther was the best thing that could ever have happened to her precious Jack, while Esther had continued to make it clear that her earlier life had required her to deal with much tougher people — even women — than Constance. They were now good friends, and 'Nanna' had even accepted that the upbringing of her grandchildren was something which she could sit back, watch and enjoy, rather than command.

Esther, for her part, had begun to slip into a comfortable middle-class existence and had even consented to join the Ladies' Guild attached to the local parish church. Although her religious education had been conducted by rabbis, she was the first to acknowledge the joint origins of Judaism and Christianity and was more than happy to lend a hand in the 'good works' that Constance and her fellow members conducted, given how good God had been to her in guiding Jack's footsteps in her direction.

Her pride had, however, been stretched to breaking point when the ever-determined Constance had achieved her ambition of bringing Jack back to Barking, away from all those 'wicked criminals' in what she considered to be Satan's own playground, the working-class stews of East London where Jack and Uncle Percy had until recently worked alongside each other as detectives in the Metropolitan Police elite known as 'Scotland Yard'. Being Constance, she had first of all made use of her Ladies' Guild contacts to secure Jack a transfer, at Detective Sergeant level, to the somewhat under-developed Essex force. She had then used much of the remaining money from Jack's share of the family trust established by his late father to acquire the vacant house in which they were now living, a ten-minute walk from the old family home, a few doors down from the parish church.

Esther's first proud impulse had been to refuse the gift and berate Constance for her condescension, but then wiser counsels had prevailed inside her sometimes-impetuous head and she reasoned that this was their best opportunity to get out of London, with all its overcrowded evils, and bring up their children in a safe place with open spaces and fresh air. It would do Jack no harm to emerge from under the protective wing of his uncle and he was already demonstrating the robust ability that was sometimes in danger of getting lost under his still boyish charm, as he rose to the challenge of being almost a senior officer — and certainly a more experienced one — in a rural police force.

They had compromised with an agreement under which Jack and Esther would regard the house as a purchase under mortgage and make monthly repayments into the family trust funds as if they were paying it over to a bank in reimbursement of a loan, and with an interest component. By this means everyone had been satisfied and the Enright family were now the proud owner-occupants of a four-bedroom detached house on a country lane on the outskirts of a respectable Essex township.

They had come a long way from the day that she and Jack had first met, investigating the evil deeds of the nightmare they'd called "Jack the Ripper", and Esther reminded herself of how much she had to be thankful for as she set about preparing the midday meal, after smiling proudly out of the kitchen window yet again at their eldest, happily swinging in the sunshine as another train rattled past on its way down to Fenchurch Street.

If Esther was satisfied that they'd made the right move, her husband Jack was less than convinced as he read the incoming crime reports and sighed with irritation behind his desk on the second floor of the ramshackle, and already overcrowded, police headquarters building in Chelmsford's Arbour Lane. No wonder the Essex force had been eager to recruit someone with 'Yard' experience, or indeed any experience at all of detective work. The force might be one of the oldest of its type outside London, but it hadn't moved with the times and Jack wasn't simply only its second ever appointed Detective

Sergeant — he was now the *only* one, after the early retirement of his predecessor, no doubt as the result of stress.

There might once have been a time when Jack had dreamed of being the head of his own force of men, but that had been in the context of a bustling Scotland Yard, with dozens, if not hundreds, of eager, highly-trained and experienced officers who had access to seemingly limitless resources. His current 'force' consisted of two constables recently dragged out of uniform, with only the vaguest idea of how to acquire evidence when it wasn't actually dumped on the ground in front of them and with little more in the way of resources than a telegraph office by means of which they could call for assistance from elsewhere — which normally meant Scotland Yard anyway.

First, but not necessarily foremost, was Detective Constable Henry Baggot — the more senior of the two, if only in years — who would be even fatter than he currently was were it not for his weekend cricket matches. Baggot had proved his value in street brawls, in which opponents would bounce off him, or sprain their wrists in an effort to penetrate his ample gut, but he'd never quite got the message that detective work involved a subtler approach to suspects than shoving their arms up their backs and hauling them down to the cells. Baggot didn't seem to appreciate — however many times Jack reminded him — that before a suspect might be arrested, some evidence was required to justify the loss of liberty that this involved, and it was probably only a matter of time before the local force was sued for false imprisonment, assault or something similar.

Then there was Constable Billy Manvers, and Jack lived in dread of the day when he was required to advise Billy's young wife that she was now a widowed single mother of two, such was Billy's over-enthusiasm to prove his worth by boldly confronting even those villains who conducted business with firearms. He'd been hospitalised twice during Jack's few brief months at Chelmsford — once with a gunshot wound that was fortunately only to the left arm. For all his eagerness, Billy also failed to appreciate that detective work was a longer-term waiting game, quietly accumulating something called 'evidence'. Jack had learned that the hard way from Uncle Percy, he reminded himself, and he could only aspire to be as good a mentor to Billy as Percy had been to him.

As Jack shifted through the papers on his desk, he was unsurprised to discover that several more families in rural Essex had been deprived of the contents of their garden sheds, washing lines and outhouses during the past twenty-four hours. It all seemed to be the work of the same person or persons who'd been at it for weeks now and must surely have cornered the market in garden forks, spades and bags of fertiliser. Perhaps he'd send Harry Baggot to investigate — on foot, in the hope of reducing his girth. Of marginally more interest was last night's fight in the Black Swan (the 'Mucky Duck', as the locals called it), in which two of the town's less worthy citizens had fought themselves to a standstill before being heaved out of the wreckage of what had formally been the public bar by two uniformed constables. One of them was Robert ('Mad Rab') Prescott, so one could anticipate a 'payback' rematch between Rab's wife Martha and the rarely sober 'common law' spouse of the loser, Ted Price, who would at least have to take time out from her usual occupation of shoplifting from grocery stores.

Finally, there was an alleged rape in the deserted windmill at Great Dunmow, which Jack quickly lost interest in when he spotted the name of the victim. If Clara Bristow had been subjected to intercourse without her consent, he concluded, then it could only have been because the alleged offender hadn't paid in advance, and he wasn't about to waste valuable police time on a case that the jury would throw out once Clara's previous convictions for loitering for the purposes of prostitution were revealed by a grinning defence barrister.

That left Jack with the simple task of deciding which train to catch home later that afternoon. He had to choose carefully, if he wanted to make the necessary connection that no-one had mentioned when his mother had gleefully announced that his new house was 'convenient for the station'. It was not, however, so convenient for the trains, since in its enthusiasm to provide a swift service from Fenchurch Street to Tilbury and Southend, the London, Tilbury and Southend Railway Company had declined to be delayed by diverting to Chelmsford. The trains certainly ran every half hour at busy times, but if he wanted to travel by train from Barking to Chelmsford, Jack was required to change at Pitsea, to catch a Great Eastern Railways train that would complete his journey to work on a better class train that had left Liverpool Street on its way to Norwich.

He'd just decided that he could justify catching the 'up' Norwich to Liverpool Street express train that left shortly after four, which connected nicely with a local train that would get him home in enough daylight to water his tomato seeds under glass beneath the kitchen window, when there was the usual heavy thump on the door that announced the imminent arrival of Harry Baggot. Out of breath with uncharacteristic excitement, Harry lost little time is delivering the news.

'They've found another baby's body, Sarge — in the Thames, this time.'

Jack sighed. The third in as many months, and he'd need to take charge of this one himself.

Chapter Three

'Do you think we've laid out enough pieces of fruit cake?' Esther asked Constance as they stood surveying the tea table in the church hall, ahead of the meeting.

'Almost certainly, dear,' Constance replied with a nod, 'but you'd better check that Mary filled the tea urn to capacity before she turned on the gas. It's quite a warm day, and there'll be lots of demand for drinks, I suspect.'

It was the monthly 'outreach' meeting of the Ladies' Guild and the vicar's wife, Clarice Spendlove, had arranged for a guest speaker whose address to the members was being eagerly anticipated, given all the recent scandal regarding the prosecution of a bookseller in London's Tottenham Court Road for stocking the 'wicked' volume entitled *The Fruits of Philosophy, or the Private Companion of Young Married People* by American physician Charles Knowlton, in which he not only advocated contraception within marriage, but actually gave practical advice on the methods available.

Since Knowles was an unashamed Atheist, his publication was shunned by Anglican communities such as that which attended Barking's St Margaret's Church. However, the somewhat more progressive vicar's wife, who had four children of her own and had no wish for any more, had invited Sister Grace, the 'Superintendent' of the Anglican Order that ran the 'Holy Heart' Orphanage, up the road in Brentwood, to inject a little humanitarian realism into the debate by enlightening the members of the influential Ladies' Guild regarding the realities of life for orphans and other unwanted children.

Sister Grace, accompanied by a beaming Clarice Spendlove, rose from the table at the front and smiled appreciatively at the spattering of applause. After clearing her throat, she began her address in a clear high voice that was almost child-like and contradicted the forty odd years suggested by the slightly lined face under the cowl.

'First of all, my thanks to Mrs Spendlove, and your committee, for the kind invitation to address you today, and for so many of you for turning out on what promises to be a rather hot Spring afternoon. Let me reassure you that I'm not here on a fundraising campaign, although should any of you wish to donate to the work of Our Lord in tending to the needs of His tragically abandoned children in our modest orphanage, then I've left certain literature with Mrs Spendlove on how you may do so.

'At the last count we had eighty-seven children in the Holy Heart, but we could have five times that number if we had the buildings and other facilities. The sad fact is that we live in an age of over-population, and while I do not wish to descend into the somewhat controversial topic of birth control, or contraception as doctors call it, the fact remains that many children born these days are neither planned for nor, regrettably, even wanted. I'm not simply referring to what polite society calls "fallen women", who are forced to trade their bodies for the bare essentials of life, but to the thousands upon thousands of "unwanted" children at every level of our modern society, whether we look at the overburdened wives of successful professional men who cannot employ nursemaids and governesses in sufficient numbers, or whether we consider the honest hardworking creatures of toil in our factories and shops, or those seeking to otherwise support their legitimate children long after they have ceased to receive support from the fathers who sired them.'

At this point Sister Grace paused for a sip of water from the tumbler in front of her on the trestle table, before continuing.

'Whatever their origins, these unfortunate children of God who cannot be nursed and fed by their mothers — many of whom are heartbroken to part with them — find their way into sanctuaries such as the Holy Heart, where they can at least be clothed, fed and educated, before we are obliged to send them out into the world in order to make way for the many others who are waiting to be received, and who would otherwise die in the gutter, or fall prey to wicked evil, in the unforgiving streets of our towns and cities.

'We have benefitted much from the same legislation that provided for the Board Schools that many of your own children will be attending. Because we provide an education of sorts — domestic training for the girls, rudimentary factory skills for the boys, and reading and writing for all — we receive an annual grant from the county authorities that allows us to employ teachers from outside, many of whom work for the pittance which is all we can allow them in return for supplying our children with the bare essentials for the harsh existence that awaits them once they leave our care, the girls at fourteen and the boys a year older than that. Yes, the lady in the blue hat?'

'What happens to your children when they leave you?' Mrs Blenkinsop enquired.

Sister Grace spread out her arms in a gesture of ignorance.

'We are not at present able to keep track of their ultimate fates, but I know of at least two who have repaid God's mercy by returning to us in holy orders to assist in the continuation of our work. Others occasionally visit us to thank us for what we did for them, and some of those are accompanied by their own children, happily loved and well nurtured. But regrettably I suspect that others fall by the wayside and become either gin-sodden and downtrodden domestic slaves or fallen women of the type which are all too familiar in and around our licensed dens of iniquity. As for the boys, some become respectable workmen, farmers and suchlike, while perhaps inevitably there are others who take to crime. I know of at least one who was hanged, and when I remember his bright, shiny eager face at the age of seven, when I introduced him to the Gospels, it breaks my heart... Forgive me.'

She'd been obliged at this point to tug a handkerchief from the sleeve of her garment and press hard to stop the tears from flowing more freely down her face. There was an awkward silence before she looked back at Clarice Spendlove and nodded encouragingly.

'Any further questions? I'm sure there are many, so please don't be shy about asking them.'

'Where do your children come from?' enquired Mrs Ingoldsby.

'All over the district,' was the reply, 'although with the gradual encroachment of heavy industry along the Thames Estuary, we find that we're taking more from townships like Dagenham and Tilbury.'

'My question was more along the lines of how the children come to be presented at your door,' the questioner persisted. 'Are they abandoned on your doorstep?'

Sister Grace smiled indulgently. 'I'm afraid Mr Dickens has a lot to answer for in the modern-day image of orphanages such as ours. The occasional one is found lying outside our chapel, certainly, but the vast majority are brought in by their mothers, in a desperate state of grief and despondency, or perhaps by someone who's found them lying by the roadside or has hastily removed them before one or other of the parents could do away with them in the last stages of despair.'

Constance Enright was surprised and a little alarmed when Esther rose quickly from her seat at this point and scuttled hastily out of the church hall, cramming her handkerchief to her mouth and making choking noises. Constance waited until the formal part of the meeting was over and Sister Grace was surrounded by eager questioners who were holding teacups in one hand and plates of fruitcake in the other, before going in search of her daughter-in-law. She found Esther in the churchyard, seated on the bench donated by a local landowner half a century earlier, situated between his tombstone and that of several of his former retainers. As Constance called her name, Esther looked up, her face red and blotchy with tears, and began to offer an apology for her abrupt departure. Constance sat down next to her and placed a consoling hand on her shoulder.

'No need to apologise, dear. I'm just delighted that you're not unwell. I thought perhaps that you'd had a sudden attack of nausea.'

'No, nothing like that,' Esther reassured her in a throaty voice still thick with emotion. 'It was when the speaker mentioned women coming to her orphanage in the final stages of desperation, heartbroken at having to part with their children. I just started thinking about my three and how it must feel to have reached that point at which you have to hand them over. Something came over me, I'm afraid. Thank God I've got Jack and that we're financially secure!'

'I don't think I've seen you so emotional since your wedding day, dear,' Constance smiled comfortingly, 'but if you feel so strongly about the matter, perhaps you should speak to Sister

Grace with a view to running a stall for the orphanage at the Summer Fair, to raise money for their wonderful work.'

'I think I might like that,' Esther smiled palely, 'but before I do I'll need to stop getting so easily upset — anything seems to start me off these days.'

'So, it wasn't just all the sad things that Sister Grace had to tell us about needy children?'

'No, that was just one instance. Last week, for example, I was out at the Post Office with Miriam in the pram, and Lily and Bertie trotting along beside me, when I saw this newspaper advertising board for the early evening edition papers that had this big headline on it, all about what it called a "Rail Disaster on the Southend Line". I immediately thought it might be the train Jack had taken to work that morning and even when I bought the paper and realised that it wasn't, I couldn't stop my mind going over and over how I'd have felt if it had been. I was a complete blubbering mess by the time we got home, and the children must have thought I was ill or something.'

'Sounds to me as if you should be consulting the doctor,' Constance advised her with a concerned look. 'Perhaps you're working too hard in that lovely house of yours. I know how particular you are, and the house is a credit to you, but perhaps you should think of hiring a domestic.'

'Most people along our road have them, I know,' Esher conceded, 'but I can't bring myself to hire someone. Jack's suggested it more than once, but I can't seem to stop telling myself that keeping house is my job and nobody else's.'

'That stubborn pride of yours will get you into serious difficulties one day,' Constance advised her with a smile, 'but for the time being, at least consult the doctor about these emotional attacks. Now, would you like some tea? I'm sure there's still some fruitcake left.'

Jack spread the case reports across his desk and looked in vain for some connection. Three infant corpses, three different methods of disposal, three different locations and three different days of the week. The latest one dumped in the Thames, where, if he was lucky, it might have floated downriver from higher up, preferably in the Met's patch. If not, then perhaps thrown in from a boat, or simply pushed into the outgoing tide from the shoreline. At least he could go and make enquiries as to whether or not anyone living in the village that overlooked the mudflat had seen anything suspicious.

The mortuary report was about as useful as an umbrella in a hurricane. The infant had been male, aged approximately two months, wrapped in nondescript, if poor, baby clothes, but no obvious cause of death. A cheerful side note from the examining physician advised him of the various ways in which a baby could be disposed of without any trace being evident once a couple of days had passed. Chloroform he could probably have guessed at, but laudanum? Wasn't that what their mothers took to take the edge off their miserable existences? Starvation was obvious, but according to the good doctor, who had probably never had to bring up a child of his own, the application of laudanum would also subdue an infant's appetite and thereby suppress its bawling for food. If given to excess it might also induce drowsiness to the point of what was described as 'cessation of voluntary respiration', which presumably meant that the poor mite gave up the effort of breathing. Finally, when Jack read that a hatpin through the heart was also swift and foolproof, he'd seen enough, and threw the report down onto the desktop with an expression of disgust.

He forced himself to read the other two reports, but carefully avoided any 'helpful' notes from the examining physician called in to the police mortuary down the road. The first case had been almost two months ago, when a farmer near Rivenhall, while emptying the last of the winter cattle feed from his storage shed, had found the skeletal remains of what he first thought was a dead animal, until he took a second look at the arrangement of the limbs, which were clearly infant arms and legs rather than the four legs of a dog or cat. The corpse had been naked and according to the best guess of the police surgeon, it was female, probably around three months old, and probably placed there once the first of the bales had been positioned on the ground. Jack was working on the theory that it had in fact been dead for some time before being concealed in the shed, and he could at least go through the motions of interviewing farm labourers to enquire if any of them could assist with the timing of that possible dumping.

A month after that came the second in what had then officially become a 'series'. A foul smell from the dustbins in the rear yard of the 'Dog and Pheasant' in Harlow had been investigated by its landlord for long enough for him to call in the local police. In a classic case of 'pass the parcel', another twenty-four hours elapsed before the badly decomposing remains had become the responsibility of a complaining police surgeon. He could be forgiven for not having spent any longer on the examination than he needed to, and his somewhat sketchy report revealed the victim to have been two to three months old, male, and with a badly deformed leg as the result of injuries that were almost certainly sustained at birth, given the signs of incomplete healing.

Someone was clearly in the habit of disposing of unwanted babies, that much was obvious. The more difficult question was whether it was all down to one person, dumping three infant corpses in three different locations to cover their tracks, or three separate callous disposals by three separate people.

There was a hesitant tap on his office door — which at least ruled out Harry Baggot — and standing in the doorway was the young constable from the front desk.

'There's a Miss Bristow downstairs, wanting to know when she's to come in and give us a statement regarding the afternoon she was assaulted.'

'Have you run out of pens and ink down there or something?' Jack demanded grumpily.

The boy looked embarrassed as he replied, 'We tried that, sir, but she's insisting that she'll only talk to a detective. Reckons that nobody in uniform would be likely to believe her, since she's been through here a couple of times for tottying.'

'And what makes her think that the Detective Branch will be any more gullible? Tell Detective Constable Manvers to take her statement, try not to laugh, then throw it in the paper basket.'

'Sick leave, sir.'

'Pardon?'

'He's on sick leave, apparently. I thought you'd been told.'

'What is it this time? A broken neck, or just a dented pride?'

'Sprained ankle, sir. Chasing a burglar across a roof, then jumped down to try to cut him off and landed badly.'

Jack sighed loudly. 'Tell Miss Bristow to make sure she gets payment in advance in future. Then tell her I'm too busy investigating three dead babies.'

'Don't let Bertie eat any more birthday cake,' Esther called out to Jack as he wandered towards the dining table on which the goodies were laid out for little hands to grab at them. 'If he has any more I'll be wiping it off his bedroom carpet at three in the morning.'

They had all finished playing polite games and were now enjoying what they had really come for. The dozen or so children that made up the celebration party for Bertie's fourth birthday were a noisy mixture of immediate family and hand-picked local Board School friends of Lily's. Hand-picked by her grandmother Constance, that is, and therefore guaranteed to be well-bred, quietly behaved and suitably grateful.

'Come for more strawberry jelly?' Uncle Percy enquired sarcastically as he slipped two sausage rolls into his jacket pocket and made a pretence of reaching for more carrot sticks.

Jack grinned. 'We're supposed to nick sleight-of-hand merchants, not learn their tricks of the trade.'

'Just don't tell your Aunt Beattie,' Percy requested, 'else I'll be back to rabbit food for another week.'

'I'm too busy policing my son,' Jack replied with a nod towards where Bertie was hovering near what was left of the birthday cake that had been ceremonially cut half an hour previously and was now drying out nicely on its cardboard base, its four candles lost somewhere in memory. 'Esther reckons he's had enough.'

'How's life among the yokels of Essex?'

'Increasingly urbanised,' Jack advised him without the hint of a smile. 'The crime's the same as in the Met, except there's not so much of it. But with a Detective Branch of only three, the odds are roughly the same, so no change really. Does anyone miss me back at the Yard?'

'Apart from me, you mean? No idea. And you're missing nothing, believe me.'

'I wasn't thinking of applying for a transfer,' Jack advised him with a smile. 'For one thing, it's too early to come back with my tail between my legs, and for another, all that political stuff was beginning to lose its appeal.'

'There's no guarantee you'd be allocated to the Political Branch even if you *did* come back,' Percy replied, as he lifted his lemonade glass high in the air to protect it from a passing child doing train impersonations. 'It's all got very routine and there's talk of reducing manpower and transferring men back into general duties.'

'Not you, I hope?'

'No, although unless the Queen takes to shoplifting in Marshall and Snelgrove, or the Prime Minister gets apprehended accosting totties in Whitechapel, I may find it difficult to justify my current rank without transferring out. Nothing you could offer me to prevent that dreaded day, I don't suppose?'

'Hardly,' Jack replied gloomily, 'unless you're experiencing a sudden increase in royal princesses falling pregnant and hiding the consequences in hay barns, pub dustbins and oyster beds in the lower Thames. I was thinking of pushing that last one your way anyway, since it may have floated downstream from somewhere on your patch.'

'It wouldn't be the first infant corpse we've pulled out of the drink lately,' Percy replied with a frown as he saw his wife Beattie strolling over to detach him from the food table. 'I'm so bored these days that I read reports coming in from all over the Met and dead babies floating around the Docks is a common theme. Send me your latest by wire and I'll see if I can find an excuse to come out and investigate.'

'I've got two more,' Jack told him as he leaned forward to kiss Aunt Beattie goodbye, 'so I'll send you those as well, shall I?'

'So long as what you're talking about isn't edible,' Beattie Enright replied starchily as she took Percy's elbow and steered him towards the door. 'And don't think I didn't notice you smuggling those sausage rolls into your pocket. They just became your tea, Percy Enright.'

Percy shot Jack a helpless look as he turned away under the firm guidance of his wife's hand on his arm. 'Send them to me and I'll see what I can do — if I haven't died of starvation, that is.'

'That'll be the day,' was Beattie's final shot. 'Whenever you get with Jack you seem to put on weight.'

Chapter Four

'We'd better finish us dinners an' get on wi' this blocked drain,' Jim Tollman instructed his young assistant John Penn as he threw the remains of his last cheese sandwich to the sparrows that were hopping hopefully in front of him on the lawn, took a last swallow of cold tea from his bottle and stood up. John, eager as ever, followed suit and they walked back across the lawn to the side of the terraced house in Cobham to finish the job that the landlord had hired them for.

The previous tenants had succeeded in breaching their lease because of the state of the drains, which were alleged to be almost permanently blocked, with the occasional embarrassing and nauseating tendency to 'back up' through the lavatory pan. Jim and John had already completed the obvious test of unscrewing the external 'downpipe' where it entered the sewer pipe and flushing the upstairs lavatory. The water had run clearly out onto the ground without any sign of a blockage, so the problem was somewhere along the clay pipe that ran under the lawn.

Before stopping for their dinner break, the two men had carefully dug a trench on either side of the pipe, which now lay exposed to the air. There was a disagreeable smell in the general area of a connecting clamp and they opted to begin with that. While Jim stood with one foot on either side of the clamp, inside the three-foot trench, and John leaned down from just above him, they tried to unscrew it several times, but with no success. Finally, Jim lost patience and looked back up at John.

'Take yer 'ammer an' gi' a firm whack on the clamp, ter see if yer can loosen it. Not too 'ard, mind, else yer'll bust it.'

Doing as instructed, John began hitting the clamp with his joiner's hammer, increasing the strength of his blows with each attempt.

'I think yer loosenin' it, boy,' Jim told him encouragingly. 'Gi' it one more — a bit 'arder this time.'

John tried to reposition himself for a heavier blow, but at the crucial moment his boot slipped on the muddy edge and his blow landed, not on the junction clamp, but on the clay pipe that was joined to it on the 'house' side of the junction. There was a sickening crack and a spout of foul-smelling liquid shot up and hit John in the face, while splattering Jim's trousers and boots. As the crack widened under the pressure of what had been jammed underneath for some time, bits of clothing, lumps of decomposing flesh and the occasional bone bubbled out from inside.

As the first tiny skull appeared, Jim began blaspheming, while John rushed into the shrubbery to disgorge his dinner.

Chapter Five

'Persuade me, if you can, how this might be justified as part of your work in the "Political Branch", Detective Inspector,' Chief Superintendent Bray demanded with an expression of pure scepticism as he lounged back in the chair behind his office desk.

From the chair across the desk Percy Enright frowned. 'As for what you call my "work" in the Political Branch, I don't currently have any,' he replied, adding, 'and I say that with considerable reluctance, in case you reallocate me to directing traffic around Trafalgar Square or something.'

'Fat chance of that,' Bray smiled back. 'There are too many eating houses in that vicinity to be able to rely on you not to wander off and cause the traffic smash of the decade. But surely you must have *something* to work on, or have we been too successful in our objective to suppress public scandals?'

He was at least admitting the carefully obscured agenda of the subtly titled 'Political Branch', which had nothing to do with politics, but everything to do with ensuring that the image of Victoria's government and immediate family remained officially unsullied, by the careful process of preventing the commission of crime by persons in the public eye and covering up the ones they didn't get to in time.

'The last job I did any work on was that sordid business involving the Senior Butler at Clarence House,' Percy admitted.

Bray nodded. 'Great job, that.'

'I've done nothing since except draw my pay and peruse reports from all over the Met. My wife tells me that I'm getting fat.'

'And she's quite correct in that, Percy,' Bray smiled. 'But before I allow one of my best smoothers-over of high-class indiscretions to go back to buckling Petermen and investigating bank frauds, I clearly need to find something to occupy you in the Political Branch. Perhaps I could arrange to be seen leaving a Molly House or something.'

'No more Molly houses, please,' Percy winced. 'We closed down most of the worst of them following that Oscar Wilde business, and believe me when I assure you that I've seen enough men in women's clothing to last me a lifetime. But there *is* a political dimension to what I'm seeking your permission to investigate.'

'Dead babies?' Bray enquired disbelievingly.

Percy nodded. 'Precisely. Why do you think we're suddenly getting a spate of dead babies?'

'Somebody's killing them, obviously,' Bray replied with heavy sarcasm.

Percy took a deep breath before persisting. 'But why?'

'Obviously their mothers didn't want them.'

'Then why are they being born in the first place, and who's doing away with them?' Percy demanded with a victorious smile.

'Shouldn't we be more concerned with your second question?' Bray demanded. 'It's our job to find the abortionists and lock them away.'

'From what I've been reading in the dozens of reports currently littering my desk,' Percy replied, 'these corpses weren't of aborted babies. Most of them, according to the police doctors who examined the remains, were at least a few weeks old before they were snuffed.'

'So?'

'So, we're not dealing with abortionists,' Percy replied patiently, resigned to spelling it out for the benefit of a senior officer who'd probably last seen a real crime when he'd passed off a weekend in a holiday resort on the Sussex coast with his wife as a liaison visit to a rural force. 'We're dealing with people, and one assumes that they're women, who take mature infants — in the sense that they've been alive for a week or two — then dispose of them, presumably for a fee. I'm told that it's called "baby farming", sir, and we have a few case histories of that. Margaret Waters in Brixton, for one. They reckon she accounted for twenty or so in her time, and they hanged her at Horsemonger Lane almost thirty years ago.'

'Don't remind me,' Bray shuddered. 'I was a beat constable in that area at the time and was one of those detailed to guard her as she went back and forth from her prison to her trial. If we hadn't surrounded her coach the mob would have dragged her out and strung what was left of her up to dry.'

'Precisely, sir,' Percy enthused as he pressed home his advantage. 'It could be regarded as a public order priority to nip any more in the bud.'

'She was a one-off, wasn't she?' Bray queried, 'And didn't Parliament pass some Act or other to prevent it ever happening again?'

Percy shook his head. 'Parliament certainly made an effort to clean up the adoption racket, but we're not talking about adoption, sir. The orphanages are crammed to capacity, the Workhouses are bulging at the seams, and there simply aren't enough decent middle-class couples around who want to adopt. There's still a huge need for someone to take unwanted babies off the hands of their despairing mothers, and that's where women like Margaret Waters swim just below the surface, stalking the unwary or the desperate. And it didn't end with Margaret Waters, I can assure you, sir. Nor is it confined to London, as you'd expect. I assume that you read the papers?'

'Of course I do,' Bray retorted, 'and presumably you're about to remind me about Amelia Dyer?'

'I was, but it would seem that I don't need to. She'll be going on trial at the Bailey next month, and I heard a rumour to the effect that she may have done for four hundred of the poor little beggars. Four hundred, sir! No wonder they're calling her "The Ogress of Reading".'

'Yes, leave the hyperbole and emotion to the newspapermen, Percy, and tell me how all this might be classed as "political", rather than ordinary run of the mill policing.'

'Back to my first point, from which we were diverted,' Percy reminded him. 'The babies that are being disposed of are unwanted, agreed?'

'Of course,' Bray replied testily. 'So what?'

'These miserable mothers don't want their babies, or at least they can't afford to keep them, whether for financial reasons or because they can't face the scandal.'

'Get to the point, Percy.'

'Well, if you read the newspapers, then like me you'll have read of that bookseller in Tottenham Court Road who was pinched for stocking a book on how to prevent babies.'

'Quite rightly, too,' Bray sniffed.

Percy nodded. 'But whatever your position on "birth control", as it's politely called, you have to agree that, to judge by the letters to the newspapers following that prosecution, it's a political hot potato.'

'So? Where is this leading us?'

'So how long before those who advocate birth control point to all these dead babies as an indication of the social evils that can be prevented if we allow it? How long before some smart politically inclined columnist writes in *The Times* that the Government is responsible for all these dead babies because of its opposition to birth control?'

'I finally see where all this is heading,' Bray conceded. 'But you aren't going to put a stop to politically embarrassing newspaper comment on birth control simply by buckling a few baby farmers, are you?'

'No — but if we can put a stop to it, we deprive these muckraking Johnnies of one bow that they can draw against the Government. Surely it's only a matter of time before the Home Secretary invites you up to Whitehall and grills you on the subject of dead babies — wouldn't you like to be in a position to inform him that you have your best man on it?'

Bray contemplated the ceiling for a brief while, while Percy held his breath. Eventually the silence was broken as the senior officer spoke to the chandelier. 'You've got a month to demonstrate progress, and three months to come up with some names.'

'Six months to buckle them, and a year to see them swing?' Percy added.

Bray nodded. 'Don't let me down, Percy. I've only got a couple of years left until my retirement.'

Esther alighted from the horse bus, took a welcome breath of fresh air and walked down the street until she came to the sombre building with a brass plate on its front entrance that advised her that she was about to enter the 'Holy Heart Orphanage'. She'd put it off for long enough and her letters back and forth to Sister Grace had only been of sufficient use to confirm that the children would no doubt benefit enormously from whatever money Esther could raise by manning — and indeed supplying — a cake stall at the forthcoming St Margaret's 'Summer Fayre', to employ the archaic spelling that seemed to have become permanent. Now it was a matter of talking over the final detail and looking the children over in the somewhat condescending belief that the presence of one or two of them around the cake stall would promote sales.

The door chime was followed by the sound of monastic boots walking purposefully down a flag-stoned corridor, then the door opened and a beaming fresh-faced woman of approximately Esther's own age smiled out at her from under her white cowl.

'I'm Mrs Enright,' Esther explained, 'I believe that Sister Grace is expecting me.'

'Indeed she is,' the woman confirmed. 'Please follow me.'

Esher was shown into a large panelled room that had a long table in its centre, a slightly threadbare carpet, a collection of pen and ink drawings of saints and martyrs on the walls, and a view of a garden beyond the large windows to one side. Sister Grace was not alone as she rose to welcome Esher into her domain and introduce her to the other woman, a lady in her late forties, Esther estimated, dressed in ordinary 'street' clothing.

'This is Margaret Meacher, one of our towers of strength,' Sister Grace enthused. 'Without her tireless devotion we'd need at least two more in holy orders to conduct the many and varied tasks that she performs with such dedication and skill. I thought, if you don't mind, that she could show you around and assist you to choose two children for your cake stall, then we can all meet up again in here for afternoon tea.'

That seemed to be beyond any possible disagreement, so Esther smiled gracefully as Margaret Meacher led her out of the Superintendent's office and into a corridor down which could be heard loudly shouted instructions coming from an open door halfway down.

'That's the senior girls' cooking class,' Margaret advised her. 'I'm hoping to be invited to take that myself when Sister Mercy's too old, which won't be long, I imagine. She does the cooking for the whole orphanage and I often assist her, so I know that sometimes she finds it all a bit much.'

'Have you been associated with the orphanage for long?' Esther enquired politely as they walked down the corridor towards the classroom.

'Over twelve years now,' Margaret replied proudly. 'I first became associated with it when I was able to bring them a few children who'd been abandoned by their mothers and who were being looked after by a lady I knew from my days behind the counter in the Post Office in Braintree. That was when my husband was the Postmaster, then after he died I moved to my cottage in Witham and lost contact with the lady who so kindly looked after the orphans before passing them to me. But by then I was a regular here and sensing my own personal loneliness Sister Grace very kindly let me work here whenever my own health permits, which is most of the time. Anyway, here we are.'

The cooking class was halted for long enough for Esther to be introduced to Sister Mercy and explain her mission. The elderly nun nodded towards a tall girl with red hair sticking out from under her institution cap.

'That's Nell, who's our best baker and sometimes helps me with the daily loaf bake. She'd be ideal for a cake stall, I imagine, and since she's thirteen now, she won't be with us much longer.' She raised her voice and called out to the girl. 'Nell, my love, would you be willing to help this lady here —

Mrs Enright — at a cake stall she's going to be running at her local church fair, to raise money for the orphanage?'

'Yes, Sister,' Nell replied eagerly, 'and if you need more than one, can we take Billy along as well?'

Sister Mercy smiled indulgently and lowered her voice to speak to Esther.

'Billy's her "special friend", shall we say? He's a year older than her and he'll therefore be leaving at the same time as her next year. I wouldn't be surprised to hear of an early wedding there, but of course while they're living here there's none of that sort of thing allowed. You'll find Billy in the carpentry shop, and don't take any cheek from Bert Hemmings.'

Ten minutes later Esther had added Billy Thorpe to her sales team for the church fair and had politely declined his instructor Bert's offer to come along with him and construct the finest table a churchyard had ever seen. For the next half hour or so she admired the clean, if very functional, dormitories, bathrooms and games room, and had made a mental note of the design of the lattice work waiting to hold up the tomatoes that were already well above ground level in the rudimentary greenhouse. Then it was time for the promised afternoon tea, and Sister Grace was anxious to know what Esher had made of it all.

'Very impressive,' Esther smiled. 'Were my own children to be orphaned, I'd be content to know that they were being so well cared for.'

'Thank you, my dear. It's so gratifying to get such a positive endorsement of all our efforts. How many children do you have?'

'Three, at present,' Esher advised her. 'A girl of five, a boy who just turned four a couple of weeks ago, and another girl, coming up to a year old, and just starting to stand upright. Hopefully there won't be too many more.'

'That's all in God's good hands, of course,' Sister Grace purred, 'and some women are never blessed with children, while others — as we know only too well here — give birth to them in the most unfortunate circumstances. It sometimes doesn't seem fair, does it? Take Margaret here. I'm sure she won't mind if I tell you — although she may already have told you herself — that she had two of her own, both taken by God before they were a year old. It happens a lot, of course, but I always think what a tragedy it is that someone so obviously loving as Margaret wasn't commissioned by God to bring up her own children.'

'That's why I was content to bring those waifs and strays here,' Margaret explained. 'I thought seriously about adopting one of them, but then my husband began his own lengthy illness and I was required to nurse him while looking after the Post Office and the little shop that went with it, so it was obviously meant.'

'Simon Peter was one of yours, wasn't he?' Sister Grace said.

Margaret nodded. 'Yes, he was my first. According to the woman who'd been looking after him, he was born to a woman in Rivenhall who was in the grip of the terrible Demon Drink and couldn't be trusted to look after the poor wee mite after her man ran out on her. I never knew his real name.'

'We were the ones who called him "Simon Peter",' Sister Grace explained for Esther's benefit. 'A nice Biblical name for a sweet fair-haired angel. Anyway, Margaret, I mentioned him because he'll be leaving us next year, with the official name of "Simon Peters" and he wants to do farm work. I thought you might know some farmer who could give him a start.'

'I'll certainly ask around,' Margaret assured her. 'But now, if you'll excuse me, I promised Sister Claire that I'd help with some sewing.'

'Yes, of course, dear — and God bless you.' Sister Grace smiled as Margaret stood up to leave and Esther decided that her departure was also probably appropriate. With many exchanges of good wishes and thanks, and a promise to return in the course of the next few weeks to meet again with Nell and Billy, Esther was escorted to the front door, from where she walked down to the stop and waited for the scheduled bus back to Barking.

As the vehicle pulled away, heading for home, where Esther could retrieve her own children from Nanna's tender care, she thought about the difference between the lives led by the orphanage children and the loving, caring, supportive family life of her own three. Was it because she had once been an orphan herself that she felt so deeply for these children? Would it be so bad if she took each one of them in turn and gave them a warm reassuring cuddle?

Cursing her own weakness and the mind that seemed to have a will of its own, she rested her head on the bus window in the front row, her face safely hidden from the several old ladies who were sharing the journey with her and allowed the tears their freedom as they rolled down her face.

Chapter Six

'Uncle Percy!' Jack yelled with delight as he stepped quickly from behind his desk and shook his visitor's hand when he was shown in by the constable from the downstairs enquiry office.

'Detective Inspector Enright to you.' Percy grinned as he took the seat in front of Jack's desk and began extracting papers and files from the commodious valise that had entered the room under his armpit. 'I'm here on business.'

'Mine or yours?'

'Both. I've been looking at those reports you wired down and added them to the collection.'

'From which I take it that you have more? You did mention a few pulled out of the Thames when we were talking at the party. Did you ever get to eat those sausage rolls, by the way?'

'What was left of them,' Percy replied with a grimace of remembrance. 'A word of advice — if you're ever going to smuggle goodies from a kid's birthday party, stay away from the sausage rolls. They have this tendency to crumble horribly in your jacket pocket, and by the time I got them home they were reduced to a collection of dry flakes, a bit like old parchment, and the sausage meat from the middle was covered in fluff from my pocket.'

'I'll bear that in mind,' Jack grinned. 'But I have better news for you if you're intending to stay for dinner. They've got lamb chops on the menu downstairs, at a ridiculously low subsidised price of fourpence. I'll treat you, if you're here for long enough, and you can return the favour the next time we're dining at the Savoy.'

'If I wasn't planning on spending the day here, I am now,' Percy smiled. 'And in fact, I'll almost certainly need to, to judge by this lot.' He opened up a large sheet of paper, laid it down on the desk, then turned it to face Jack, whose eyes opened wide.

'What's this — a diagram of the Midland Railway network?'

'No — a very simplified chart of the case that I've persuaded Bray to let me work on, provided that I can start showing progress within a month. That should be easy enough, given the lead I've already got on the one in Surrey, but I was hoping that you could move me forward on the ones here in Essex.'

'I gave you all I had on those,' Jack confessed.

Percy shook his head. 'What did I teach you, Jack? Never take a witness's first statement to be their last. Every time you talk to them again, they remember something else. And when I share with you what I've already got on the others, it might ring a few more bells.'

Jack looked down mournfully at the massive diagram that Percy had drawn up. 'So how does all this work? And is this my copy?'

'One of two,' Percy replied with a smile. 'Assuming that she's not too tied down with meetings of the Women's Gossip Club, or whatever they call themselves, and now that she's no longer knee-deep in nappies, I thought we might put the old team together. The one that caught Jack the Ripper, closed down a trade union, trapped a sister murderer and rescued a long-lost niece from the clutches of a demolition gang in Bethnal Green.'

'Esther?'

'How many sharp-brained wives do you have?'

'I think you'll find that she has other priorities these days,' Jack cautioned him. 'This sort of thing was all very fine when we were cooped up in a suite of rooms in Clerkenwell, but now that we've got a garden with a swing, the daily trip up and down to Lily's school, which Bertie will be attending next year, and...'

Percy raised his hand for silence and smiled. 'Your protective instinct is commendable, Jack, but I'm not suggesting that we employ her as a decoy duck for some sort of maniac who enjoys snuffing babies. She's very good at drawing logical conclusions from the available information, pointing out connections between items, and counselling against jumping to misleading conclusions. She'd be ideal for this job, and she can of course work from home.'

Jack looked down at the confusing chart of names, locations and dates, and the different coloured pencil lines that connected them, some bearing question marks. He sighed. 'It looks like the sort of thing that Lily used to draw, then assure us that it showed the beautiful princess being found in the dark forest by the handsome prince. It's certainly a tangle and might well benefit from a third pair of eyes. But what's wrong with mine?'

Percy smiled and applied some of his acquired knowledge of human psychology. 'Do I detect the sound of a man who's jealous of his own wife?'

'Definitely not!' Jack insisted, but Percy could see that he'd found the weak spot.

'You are, aren't you? You're afraid that if I give Esther a copy of this, she'll make more progress on it than you!'

'No!' Jack insisted.

Percy smiled like a chess champion about to checkmate his opponent's king. 'Then prove me wrong. Take it home to Esther and see what she can make of it.'

'Alright, I will,' Jack replied with the sinking realisation that his uncle had got the better of him yet again. 'But aren't you going to let me have a go, first? Fair's fair, after all.'

'Why do you think I came prepared for a whole day in Essex?' Percy replied with a triumphant smile. 'What time do they serve the lamb chops?'

'For how long exactly have you been experiencing these emotional attacks?' Dr Browning enquired of a somewhat embarrassed Esther, who had finally listened to her conscience and taken the time to attend the local surgery. Constance was more than happy to spend the morning in the house in Bunting Lane, supervising a drawing competition on the kitchen table while feeding mashed potato and turnip to a contented little Miriam, and Esther had finally given in to her mother-in-law's constant unwanted advice that she should 'get herself seen to'.

'They're not exactly "attacks",' Esther explained hurriedly. 'It's just that from time to time, for no obvious reason, something really emotional grabs me, and I can't help crying. I'd describe myself as pretty hardened as a general rule, so I thought I should get myself seen to. Do you think it's all in my head, doctor?'

Philip Browning smiled. 'No, I think it may be a more basic condition than that. I see from my records that you have three children. How old's the youngest?'

'Just over a year.'

'It *is* "Mrs" Enright, I hope?'

'Of course it is, but what's that got to do with anything?'

'When was your last monthly cycle?'

'I'm not pregnant,' Esther insisted indignantly.

'Are you telling me that you haven't missed any monthlies?'

42

'No, I haven't,' Esther insisted. 'Although...'

'Let me guess. The last two or three were smaller than usual, and the blood was lighter in colour?'

'Yes, that's right, but how did you know?'

'Taken along with the sudden unexplained emotional incidents, I'd be prepared to bet that you're expecting again.' He slid a small bottle across the desk towards her. 'Take this home with you, then bring me back a sample of your urine. Then I can confirm the good news — or at least, I hope it's good news.'

'It might not be, for my husband,' Esther grinned back sheepishly.

'Then send him along to me, and I'll remind him of what caused it.' Dr Browning smiled as he rose to escort Esther to the door.

'So, do you want to give me a clue?' Jack asked as he looked down at his copy of the intricate diagram that Percy had brought with him. 'It looks pretty complicated, and what are the dates for, and why are they underlined?'

'That's the first problem,' Percy explained. 'You may have read in the papers, or perhaps the Met circulars, if they come this far out, that we — by which I mean the Yard — recently arrested a woman called "Amelia Dyer". We're pretty sure that she's good for several hundred dead babies over the past few years — although even she seems to have lost count — and we need to make sure that we're not investigating ones that she'll eventually be hanged for. It would be a wasted effort, wouldn't it?'

'But it would also allow you to cross some off the list, surely?' Jack reasoned.

Percy nodded. 'That's the second bit of bad news. By all accounts Amelia Dyer's not playing with a full deck. She has a history of being admitted to lunatic asylums from time to time — usually when it suited her to disappear during police investigations — and there's some doubt about whether or not she's now feigning insanity, to escape the rope. So even if I subject her to intense questioning, and she's able to tick a few off the list, how will I know if she's on the level?'

'But if she's prepared to nod to a few, that reduces our task, does it not?'

Percy scowled. 'I'll pretend I didn't hear that. First of all, police officers should never sign off on a convenient confession, simply because it helps them to close a file. To do so is to make it more tempting to invent, or force, a confession, and I hope I don't have to underline why that's not a good idea. Secondly, and perhaps more to the point, if you accept a false confession by "A" to a crime that was actually committed by "B", then not only does "B" get away with it, but they're free to commit more crimes of a like nature.'

'But looking at this chart,' Jack persevered, 'the dead babies have been distributed over half the south-east of England. Surely, like most criminals, this Dyer woman stuck to her own patch?'

Percy shook his head sadly. 'Regrettably not. Amelia Dyer is a much-travelled lady. She seems to have begun in Bristol, before moving to Bath, then further east into Berkshire. She was also lodging for a while in Willesden, where she did a nice line in "adoption", as she politely called it. So, it's possible that any of these on the chart — even your ones out here in Essex — were down to her.'

Jack sighed. 'Can we learn nothing from this woman?'

Percy smiled grimly. 'We can at least learn how it's done, since the woman seems to have set the agenda for future "baby farming", as it's become known. First of all, you establish either a hospital or nursing home for expectant mothers. A genuine one, with proper nursing and midwifery services. Then you undertake to find homes for the babies who, for whatever reason, are not wanted by their mothers. This is the point at which you charge what is usually called an "adoption fee". At this stage it's still perhaps applauded as a humane process and there's nothing unlawful about it, except for charging a "finding fee" to both the desperate mother *and* the childless couple anxious to adopt.'

'But how do the babies finish up dead?'

Percy smiled as he continued. 'At some point or other, the operator of the scheme finds that they have far more babies than they have eager adopters. This is when the operation is costing them serious money, with no income apart from the pathetic few shillings that the mothers can raise, perhaps with assistance from the fathers, by way of blackmail or whatever. But the person running the scheme still has a serious over-supply of babies.'

'So, they begin killing them?'

'Precisely. Perhaps the first few starve to death and the baby farmer panics and buries the evidence of what had until then been a lawful, if somewhat callous, business operation. By this means, they come to appreciate how easy it is to dump a small body. Then the penny drops that there's no need to leave them to starve to death, with the accompanying noise of screaming brats bellowing to be fed. Why not do away with them as soon as they're handed over? Amelia Dyer seems to have opted for strangulation, but a dose of laudanum will always do the trick. If you don't have any "Godfrey's Cordial" available — a nice

45

little bedtime drink that contains opium — then there's always the hatpin through the heart, which I hear tell at the rumour counter is the latest way of organising things. Then it's just a matter of disposing of the bodies, which is where we come in.'

'We? Do you want me in on all the others, or just delving as far as I can get into the Essex ones?' Jack enquired. 'And what was that about a hopeful lead in Surrey? Could it have been this Dyer woman, do you think?'

'We can't be certain,' Percy admitted, but it's at least a line of enquiry I can follow up, while you dig up — sorry, poor choice of words — "find out" what you can on *your* infant corpses. In the Surrey case I have the name, and hopefully the address, of the person who was almost certainly in residence when a drain got blocked with dead babies. It must have been around the time when Amelia Dyer was doing a roaring trade in the Reading area, but I'm taking a punt on her not needing to wander into leafy Surrey for her next client.'

'So, it's this one here on your chart, is it?' Jack enquired. 'Annabelle Grant?' When Percy nodded, Jack asked for a guided tour of the remainder and Percy duly obliged.

'First of all, you'll notice the large gap in the centre? That's in the belief that all of those listed around the edge of the page can be linked to one person at the centre of things. I look forward to the day when we can put a name in that gap, but I've left enough room for several names, should it eventuate that we're dealing with several different operators. Now, tell me where you can see links already.'

Jack was ahead of him on that, since he'd been taking long looks at it during their previous conversations. 'Shoreditch, Whitechapel, Wapping and Stepney,' he announced proudly. 'They're all in the East End, and roughly Dockside, although only one seems to have been fished out of a dock.'

'Correct,' Percy confirmed. 'That was the Wapping one, found floating in St Katherine Dock, only the morning after it was thrown in there, according to the police surgeon. I've labelled it "Wapping", since that's where it was found, but bearing in mind Wapping's proximity to Whitechapel we can't rule out the possibility that the two were linked, even though the Whitechapel baby was found in a cardboard box in a printer's warehouse in Chamber Street, just around the corner from your old station. It was also at least a month older than the one in the dock.'

'Stepney and Shoreditch might fall into the same category,' Jack pointed out. 'All four of the East End ones could have come from the same baby farm.'

'Good thinking,' Percy confirmed, 'although if so, then the person responsible for Shoreditch and Stepney had a busy night. They were both found on the same day — the fifteenth of April — and while the Shoreditch one was in a railway carriage that had spent the night in the sidings attached to the local station, the Stepney one was simply lying in a gutter in Stepney Green.'

'The buses run late at night all the way up and down Whitechapel Road,' Jack reminded him, 'so Shoreditch, Whitechapel and Stepney could easily be covered on the one night. What was the date of the Wapping one again?'

'The seventeenth,' Percy advised him. 'Little more than two weeks ago.'

'When was Amelia Dyer arrested?' was Jack's next question, and when Percy advised him that it had been 4th April, during the Easter weekend, Jack nodded. 'So, it couldn't have been her, since I assume she's been in custody ever since.'

'She certainly has,' Percy confirmed, 'but that only means that she didn't dump the corpses herself. Whether or not she created them *before* she was arrested is another question altogether, of course.'

'But as you pointed out already,' Jack reminded him with a furrowed brow, 'she was busily occupied in Berkshire and had no need to come into the East End for business, although from what I remember of life down there, she wouldn't have lacked customers.'

'Very few of whom would have been in a position to pay her fee. However, the Middlesex one might be one of hers. A builder's yard in West Drayton, baby dumped in a wheelbarrow behind a woodpile, found in late March. An easy coach ride from Reading, I would have thought.'

'So, you'll start with the Surrey one?'

Percy nodded. 'Too good to pass up. I have the name of the previous tenant, as I already mentioned, and by a stroke of good fortune she claimed to be running the place as an adoption agency. I'm hoping that the landlords can supply me with enough additional information to track her down. Is it time for those lamb chops yet?'

As Percy and Jack stood in the already lengthy queue in the dining hall, surrounded on both sides by men in police uniforms chattering loudly over recent events, one of them called out to Jack.

'Sergeant, that totty were back at the front desk, insistin' on speakin' ter yer. I told 'er that we've allocated an officer to look into 'er case, but that 'e's currently on sick leave.'

'He must have been sicker than we all thought,' Jack replied with a smile, 'because I can see his ghost further down the queue. Tell him to take her statement, then throw it away.'

'Short on manpower?' Percy asked with a grin.

Jack nodded. 'The last thing I need, given what we're going to be working on, is a totty who claims she was raped.'

'Perhaps she was,' Percy suggested. 'Even totties sometimes have days off and if she didn't consent to it, then it's still rape. And a totty might be a good source of information about all the other naughty things going on in the neighbourhood. You're going to need to use every underworld contact you can cultivate if you want to find out more about who dumped three dead babies on your patch.'

'The only things I intend to cultivate in the forthcoming months are my tomatoes,' Jack advised him. 'And as for females who can assist me with my enquiries, didn't you trick me into dragging Esther into all this?'

'That's someone else you shouldn't underestimate. Now, concentrate on fumbling for your loose change, because we're nearly at the front of the queue and it's your treat.'

'What's in that package that you brought home from work?' Esther asked Jack later that evening, once the children were in bed.

Jack frowned. 'For some reason or other, Uncle Percy thought you might be able to assist us in a case we're working on.'

'You don't work at the Yard any more. And are you saying that Percy was here in Essex without visiting me and the children?'

'He'll be there on Sunday at Mother's, so don't start feeling neglected. He came to Chelmsford specially, to add to a case he's been working on. Dead babies have been popping up all over the south-east. I've got three of my own in the county, and Percy's trying to make connections between those and a load more in places like the East End, Surrey and Middlesex.'

'He thinks they may all be the work of the same person?'

'Possibly, and he wants to use what he chooses to call your analytical brain to spot links he may have missed. In the package, which you can open tomorrow, is the chart he's made of all the known dead babies so far, with the places, times and dates. Don't let the kids draw on it, because it's the only copy you'll get.'

'He doesn't want me to go posing as a nanny or anything, I hope? Only you may have noticed the presence of children around the place who tend to occupy my full attention. Added to which, I have to organise a cake stall at the Summer Fair, in aid of that orphanage I visited recently in Brentwood.'

'At least you're dealing with live children there. You may find it a bit stressful when you have a look at the chart thing that Percy's drawn up, with all the details of infant corpses.'

Percy looked up at the signboard above the window, to check that this really was the property agency responsible for leasing out Number 17, Cedar Lane, Cobham. There was a faint tinkle from a bell above the front door as he pushed it open and walked towards the counter with his police badge held high in the air, before the middle-aged man behind it could attempt to sell him a house.

'What have we done?' the man joked nervously.

Percy smiled. 'Whatever it is, I'll find out sooner or later. But for the time being I'm interested in Number 17, Cedar Lane.'

'Ah yes, nasty business,' the man conceded. 'I'm Lionel Winters, and that property's one of mine. Under my management, I mean — the owner's serving in the army in India.'

'The previous tenant — the one who may have left a certain problem in the drains,' Percy reminded him, 'I already have a name, but presumably you have a current address?'

'Let me see now,' Winters muttered as he turned to open a filing cabinet behind him and extracted a folder labelled with the address of the house in question. 'We obviously have the address that Miss Grant gave us when she first took the lease, plus the references that she gave us at the time, but as for what might be her current address I have no idea. She could have gone anywhere after leaving Number 17, you appreciate?'

'You made no effort to locate her, after the unfortunate business with the drains?' Percy enquired.

Winters shook his head. 'No. To tell you the truth, when you people started investigating I assumed that you'd track her down. If you do, we may well commence court proceedings for the cost of the installation of new drains. No luck, I take it?'

'That's why I'm here,' Percy sighed. 'Give me the previous address at least and I'll start there.'

An hour later Percy was back, with a less than amused expression on his face.

'Did you locate her?' Winters asked.

Percy snorted dismissively. 'I certainly found the address she gave you, and either you didn't check it for yourselves, or you were visited by her ghost.'

'I beg your pardon?'

'The address you gave me in Oxshott belongs to an undertaker and has done for the past twenty years or so. Surprisingly enough, the lady I spoke to had never heard of Annabelle Grant, alive or dead. We checked their records carefully for an entry in the latter category.'

'Most unfortunate,' Winter conceded. 'We're always meticulous on checking before we let out substantial properties like that to strangers.'

'You took references?' Percy enquired cynically.

'Of course,' Winter assured him as he retrieved the file which hadn't yet been replaced in the cabinet behind him. 'Read them for yourselves. Here they are — previous landlord, and the local vicar in Oxshott.'

Percy frowned, then pushed the file back across the counter. 'Both of whom appear to have the same handwriting, Mr Winters. When and if I'm searching for a suitable property in this locality I can only hope that you have a business rival. Good day and thank you for nothing.'

Chapter Seven

Percy stood to the side of the house, kicking disconsolately at a lump of turf that had not quite settled properly after the police had finished extracting the grisly remains of at least two infants from the trench that had been dug around the sewer pipe. They had only found two skulls, but enough arms and legs to account for at least three infants, so either the third skull had been disposed of by some other means, or it been able to float freely before the pipe became blocked. There had been some cheap baby clothing, but nothing to indicate where the clothing might have originated, or to whom it may have belonged, and given that the sewer drain joined up with a larger one in the middle of Cedar Lane before discharging its foul contents, first into the nearby River Mole, then ultimately into the Thames somewhere around Hampton Court Palace, there had been no further evidence to be gained from that source. It all came down to the former resident Annabelle Grant, and she had clearly gone to some lengths to cover her tracks.

'Are you with the police?' came a voice from over the adjoining side hedge, and Percy found himself looking at a bespectacled elderly lady who had 'busybody' invisibly stamped across her forehead.

'Yes, I am,' Percy replied. 'Detective Inspector Enright, Scotland Yard.'

'The rumours are true, then? Miss Grant was murdering babies instead of arranging for their adoption?'

'So it would seem,' Percy confirmed. 'I take it that you live next door, Mrs…?'

'Talbot — and it's "Miss". Yes, this was my parents' house, and I inherited it when they died. I've just laid out some tea and crumpets on the table in the garden, so would you by any chance care to join me? You'll need to go back out into the lane to access my garden, I'm afraid, since there's no gate between the two properties. Perhaps as well, in the circumstances. When you come through the front gate, Barney will yap and jump all over your legs, but he doesn't bite.'

Hoping that 'Barney' turned out to be a dog and not the lady's brother, Percy made his way next door. Once in the rear garden he was shown to a hard-backed garden chair and served with tea and crumpets with all the grace and style normally bestowed on a customer taking afternoon tea at Claridge's. His second crumpet eagerly consumed with suitable expressions of appreciation, he began with the only prompt he needed, given the lady's eagerness to disclose all she knew to such a distinguished guest whose presence in her rear garden she could boast about to her bridge club for the foreseeable future.

'You knew Miss Grant?'

'Just to speak to across the hedge, but yes. She ran a very busy establishment next door there and could only find the time to come out for some fresh air and an elevating conversation in the late afternoons. She ran a high-class adoption agency, you know. I was *so* shocked when I learned what they'd found in the drains. She always appeared to be so *respectable*.'

'What can you tell me about her adoption business?'

'"Agency",' Miss Talbot corrected him. 'Very upper-class. No cast-offs of fallen women there, let me assure you. The clients came and went in their private carriages, for the most part, and I happened to know one or two of them, although I'm not one for gossip, as I hope you can tell.'

'Indeed, Miss Talbot. But you actually knew some of her clients by sight, you say?'

'Indeed I did, but *only* by sight. Except for Mrs Boothroyd, of course. I play bridge with her every Wednesday. Do you play bridge, by any chance? We're always looking for new mature male members.'

'No, I'm afraid not. This Mrs Boothroyd — was she adopting, or did she perhaps have a child in need of adoption?'

'I would never dream of asking her about such a delicate matter, but it's common knowledge hereabouts that she lost a child to diphtheria and was in deep mourning for some time. It was a girl, and if you attend their business premises these days — he's a chiropodist operating from home, just down the road there, and his nameplate's on the front gate — you'll notice the presence of a girl of about five or six in the garden. They do say that Ethel Boothroyd adopted the child through Miss Grant, although, as I said, I'm not one for gossip.'

'No, indeed,' Percy acknowledged with a smile, wishing that he could be blessed with witnesses like this one all the time. 'And how long had Miss Grant been gone before the people who came after her complained about the drains?'

'Only about a month or so. But they were *totally* unsuited to a property of that quality, if you ask me. Rumour had it that he was a bookmaker, and as for her — well, least said and all that. But you could tell just by looking at them that they were the sort to cause trouble, and don't we all experience problems with the drains from time to time?'

'Yes indeed,' Percy conceded, 'but the problem in this case was a bit more than your average.'

'I still can't believe it,' Miss Talbot insisted. 'She was so — so — *well-thought-of*. Have you arrested her, by any chance?'

'No, we're still looking for her, I'm afraid,' Percy advised her. 'I don't suppose you...'

'Certainly not, Inspector, and even if I did I wouldn't wish to be party to any process that led to her arrest, poor woman. So *respectable* and performing such a vital service to society. More tea?'

'No, thank you, I have to get back to work. But thank you so much for your kind hospitality — and of course such a pleasant chat.'

'You're welcome, young man. Always nice to have a conversation that's not tainted by idle gossip. You can find your own way out to the gate?'

Five minutes and six garden gates later, Percy negotiated the front entrance to the elegantly appointed private house standing in its own grounds, whose front gate nameplate revealed it to be the home and professional consulting surgery of 'Alfred Boothroyd, Chiropodic Surgeon'. An early middle-aged lady with a worried expression responded to his ringing of the handbell on the reception desk.

'Did you have an appointment? Only my husband's having a nap, since he believed himself to be free of patients this afternoon. But if it's urgent, I can always rouse him.'

'No, nothing like that, Mrs Boothroyd. It *is* Mrs Boothroyd, isn't it?'

'Yes, it is. What's your particular problem, might I ask? I'm my husband's nurse, so you can tell me.'

'Flat feet,' Percy advised her as he held up his badge, 'but that seems to go with the job.'

'Are you here on police business?' Mrs Boothroyd enquired as she suddenly turned pale.

Percy gave her the benefit of his reassuring avuncular smile. 'I am, but nothing for you to worry about. You *or* your daughter.'

'What's your business got to do with Sarah?' she demanded in a breaking voice.

'Nothing to do with her in herself,' Percy replied. 'More a matter of how she came to be your daughter.'

Mrs Boothroyd clutched the side of the counter and appeared to be about to faint, so Percy quickly suggested that she take a seat. She nodded towards the frosted glass door with the panel that said 'Surgery', and asked, 'Can we go in there, please?'

Seated in the doctor's chair, with Percy in the seat across from her, surrounded by all sorts of instruments of potential podiatric torture, the woman smiled weakly.

'This is to do with that awful business up the road isn't it? I swear before God that we acquired Sarah legitimately, and that there was no — no — no *murder* involved. I'll confess that the adoption laws weren't totally complied with, because of my husband's age, but we'd tried all the official agencies, and we were *so* desperate after Sarah — the first Sarah, that is — was taken from us that we were prepared to try anything short of actually stealing a child. We — oh God, will we lose *her* as well, now?'

She broke down completely and began sobbing loudly. Percy sat there embarrassed, uncertain what to do or say, until the surgery door was flung open and a man stood in the doorway. He was considerably older than Percy, and was in his shirtsleeves, with his trouser braces hanging from his waist. He pierced Percy with an angry glare.

'What in God's name's going on here? Who the Hell are you, and why is my wife crying?'

'I'm a police officer, Mr Boothroyd, and I was merely enquiring into the circumstances in which you came to adopt your daughter Sarah. I can assure you both that I'm not here to take her away, and I have not the slightest intention of advising the adoption authorities of anything you confide in me, provided that you co-operate all you can in the way of assisting me to find the woman who called herself Annabelle Grant.'

'You mean that wasn't her real name?' Boothroyd demanded.

Percy shook his head. 'Almost certainly not, but had she stuck to organising adoptions — even unorthodox ones such as I believe yours was — then I wouldn't be asking these questions. But, as you may have heard, there were certain dark irregularities in the final few weeks of her occupation of the house at Number 17...'

'The babies in the drains, you mean? Forgive me, but this street has a very efficient gossip network.'

'Yes, I had afternoon tea with part of it earlier today. If you'd care to comfort your wife, I'd like a little more information from you both.'

Alfred Boothroyd walked behind the desk and hugged his wife, gently rocking her in his arms until she appeared more composed. Then he took a spare chair from the corner of the surgery and placed it next to Percy's before enquiring, 'Whisky?'

'No thanks,' Percy replied with a smile, 'but don't let me stop you. My arrival here is probably quite a shock to you both.'

Alfred Boothroyd disappeared briefly, and before he returned with a cut-glass tumbler containing an impressive quantity of whisky, his wife Ethel had recovered sufficient composure to seek reassurance from Percy.

'You really *won't* report us over Sarah? She means everything to us, and if we lost her as well after all this time, it would be the end of Alf, I just know it would.'

'How long has she been with you?' Percy asked.

'Over four years now. We got her when she was just a few months old.'

'From Miss Grant, presumably?'

'Yes. She ran a very exclusive adoption agency. No children from — well, you know, "unsuitable" women. We were told that Sarah's mother was a teacher in a ladies' academy who was seduced by a teacher from an associated school who turned out to be married, and the mother was obliged to part with Sarah because her employment required her to "live in" as a housemistress in the school, which was one of those boarding type establishments. We obviously never met Sarah's birth mother, but since we got her she's demonstrated nothing but good breeding, so we've never had occasion to doubt what we were told. But is it true that Miss Grant was murdering some babies?'

'That's what we believe,' Percy confirmed, 'although that's based very largely on the fact that she was in residence at the house when the incidents occurred.'

'She did well to high-tail it out of there when she did,' Alfred Boothroyd observed sourly as he re-entered the room and sat down. 'But you'd never have guessed what she was really like from her demeanour. Always so well turned out, politely spoken and so on, as if she were selling gowns in a top West End store.'

'Actually, I think I may have seen her since,' Ethel chimed in, and as the two men turned to look at her with surprised expressions, she continued, 'What Alf said just then kind of jogged my memory. I was in a department store in Oxford

Street — or was it Bond Street? No, it was definitely Oxford Street, I remember now. The store was called "Timothy's" and it had a children's wear department where I called in to get some suitable clothing for Sarah, who'll be starting school in September. I bought quite a lot and wanted to pay by personal cheque. Because I don't have an account with that particular store, they called the senior sales assistant to the counter to approve the transaction. This woman stepped out from behind a curtain that led to some sort of office at the back and it was her, I'm pretty sure.'

'How did you react?' Percy asked.

Ethel looked slightly embarrassed. 'I'm afraid I made a bit of a fool of myself. I made a big fuss of thanking her profusely for all she'd done for us and assuring her that Sarah was turning into a beautiful young girl. She looked blankly at me and asked if she knew me. When I tried to remind her of the adoption she'd organised and said something along the lines of "My husband and I will be forever grateful, Miss Grant", she replied coldly, "You must be mistaking me for someone else — my name's Frances Dickinson." Then she approved the transaction, turned smartly around and disappeared behind her curtain.'

'You're quite sure it *was* her?'

Ethel nodded vigorously. 'We obviously got to see her several times during the adoption process and she's quite distinctive in appearance.'

'Could you describe her for me?' Percy extracted his notebook.

Ethel stared at the ceiling as she recalled the lady in question. 'She's aged about forty-five or so, quite tall and well made. Well, big-bosomed anyway. Her hair was probably once fair, but she's gone mostly grey, and she has a very distinct "cast" in one eye — the left, I seem to remember — which tends to make her look as if she's squinting sideways. Overall, a pleasant, comfortable appearance, but no raving beauty.'

'Would you recognise her if you saw her again?'

'Probably, but do I have to? It was all very embarrassing, and I haven't been back to "Timothy's" since.'

'You may not have to,' Percy assured her, 'since I can think of another way of identifying her. But there's no doubt in your mind that the woman you saw calling herself "Frances Dickinson" is in fact the same lady you first met as "Annabelle Grant", the lady who organised the adoption of Sarah and who was running the agency?'

'Not really, no. No real doubt, anyway.'

'She may not have been running the show towards the end,' her husband reminded her, before turning to Percy to explain: 'Not long before the agency closed down, there were complaints about the place lodged with the local residents' group of which I'm currently the Treasurer. Fairly mild stuff, but constant. Mainly the noise of babies crying until late into the night, carriages trundling up and down to the door at inappropriate times, and young women laughing and carrying on as they came and went from the place. The locals were quite relieved to see the back of the woman, to be honest, and we no longer had to deal with the constant letters of complaint from that dreadful Emily Talbot, who lived next door, and who had to contend with the worst of it. You might want to talk to her.'

'I already did,' Percy replied, wondering why the sweet old lady who'd served him tea and crumpets hadn't seen fit to mention the nuisance towards the end of the tenancy.

'No doubt she pointed you towards us?' Ethel Boothroyd bristled. 'She's a very malicious old gossip and never stops asking embarrassing questions about Sarah.'

'She serves nice afternoon teas, though,' Percy said, smiling, as he rose to leave.

Jack coughed involuntarily as the smoke from a dozen pipes hit his lungs like an out of control bonfire, and he took a sip of his half pint in the hope of lubricating his tonsils. Walter and Michael Missingham had done a thorough job of announcing that a detective from Chelmsford would be in attendance to collect information from them and Walter shouted for silence above the hubbub of general talk. Jack took the deepest breath he dared, given the acrid fumes by which he was surrounded, and began.

'First of all, thank you for turning out, although I doubt that many of you needed any encouragement to visit "The Anchor" before dinner time.' He allowed the laughter to subside before continuing. 'My name's Jack Enright and I'm your local Detective Sergeant. As most of you will know, Walter and Michael here had the unfortunate experience of fishing a dead baby out of the river last week, and first of all I need to know if any of you have had a similar misfortune.' There were shakes of the head all round, but Jack persevered. 'Did any of you see or hear anything unusual at? Any strangers in the village, or any out of the ordinary incidents?'

'Jed Burton went 'ome sober one night,' someone offered and there was more general laughter.

Jack smiled politely and kept going. 'It begins to look as if the dead body may have floated down from upriver somewhere — is that a possibility? From how far upriver have you known things drift down?'

'As far as the 'ouse o' Commons,' one man replied. 'I fished a box off the beach one time what 'ad writin' on it what said it 'ad once bin full o' wine fer the Members' Dinin' Room in there. No bloody wine left in it, though, the miserable stingy bastards.'

'Is it always from the north bank — never the south?' Jack asked.

There was general laughter before Walter Missingham politely explained, 'Easy ter see yer no fisherman. The way they've dredged the navigable channel's created a swing ter the north bank an' we cops all the rubbish from upstream what used ter go both ways. We tried complainin', but the Port authorities told us ter blow it out our arses. Yer wouldn't believe what we fishes outer there sometimes — clothes, umbrellas, top 'ats.'

'But no more dead babies?' Jack persisted.

'There were a dead woman one time,' a man near the back of the group advised him. 'They reckoned she were a totty from up the Docks. But that were some years since.'

'Very well,' Jack concluded. 'I've left my calling card with Mr Missingham Senior, should any of you remember anything else.'

Two hours later, back in Chelmsford, Jack alighted from his police coach to be confronted by an angry looking girl whose face gave the impression that she'd recently done three rounds with the current heavyweight champion.

'You the big detective round 'ere, are yer?' she demanded, hands on hips.

'I'm Detective Sergeant Enright, certainly,' Jack confirmed. 'And who might you be?'

'Clara Bristow. 'Er what were raped be Joe Goodman two weeks since, an' what's bin waitin' ever since that 'appy event ter 'ave me statement took. Yer gonna wait till some bastard murders me, then yer won't need ter get off yer arses ter take me statement, will yer?'

'How did you come by those bruises, Miss Bristow?'

'I bought 'em down the shops, what d'yer think, yer strutnoddy? Joe Goodman didn't just 'ave me against me will — 'e battered me stupid, an' all!'

Jack took only a moment to consider his position. While Clara's claim of rape might not stand up to scrutiny, given her history of totting, that still didn't make it lawful for someone to turn her face into a green and purple mess. And what had Percy reminded him about needing to keep well in with low types, in the hope of getting information regarding the actions of the dregs of society? Time to heed advice that came from years of experience.

'Tomorrow's Friday, Miss Bristow, and we're normally kept pretty busy on pay day. But if you come in on Monday morning at, say, ten o'clock, I'll take your statement personally. How would that suit?

''Bout time,' Clara grumbled as she walked away.

Jack walked up to his office in the hope that somewhere in headquarters they kept copies of tide timetables and flow charts of the Lower Thames. He also needed to telegraph to Percy at the Yard.

At the end of another frustrating day he threw his hat towards the peg on the inside of the back door at home, then bent down to pick it off the mat when he missed as usual. He looked up and saw Esther, in her best gown, smiling lovingly at him from the open kitchen door, from which a delicious smell of roast lamb was wafting.

'So, I missed the peg as usual, but why the welcoming smile, why the best dress and why roast lamb on a Thursday? Have you bought a new hat or something?'

'Later,' Esther said, smiling. 'Just come inside and get your boots off before I serve supper. The children have had theirs,

Miriam's already asleep, and Bertie soon will be, if he knows what's good for him. As for Lily, she's down at Nanna's and will be spending the night there.'

'If I didn't know better, I'd say you were setting out to seduce me.' Jack grinned as he put the fourth slice of roast lamb onto the end of his fork.

'Why would I need to seduce the most sexually persistent man in Barking?' Esther smiled back from across the table. 'If you want to ask a sensible question, try me on that diagram thing of Percy's that you left for me to study.'

'You've solved the crimes unaided?'

Esther shook her head. 'No, but something occurred to me when I was looking at the ones from the East End. I need to speak to Uncle Percy about it.'

'Why not me?'

'You as well, and preferably at the same time. But it's not like when we were living in Clerkenwell and he could just pop round at the end of the working day bearing fish and chips. We only get to see him at Sunday dinners down the road at your mother's, and you know how she disapproves of you and Percy talking about work.'

'Well,' Jack smirked back, 'you must have been inside my head earlier today when I wired him with a suggestion that he and Aunt Beattie come back here after Sunday dinner and spend the night with us, before catching a train home on Monday morning. I need to pass on some information to him and no doubt he'll have progress to report by now. We might have to make it a regular arrangement, although I suggest that we don't tell Mother. Beattie won't mind us talking shop while she plays with the kids.'

'Perfect. Now you go and put your feet up while I clear up in here.'

'Don't you want a hand with the washing up?' Jack enquired, more convinced than ever that Esther must have overspent at the local drapery shop, but Esther shook her head.

'Just go and relax, Jack. I could see by your face as you walked down from the front gate that you'd had a bad day.'

'*Every* day's a bad day at present,' he complained, 'and the sooner I can get away from thinking about dead babies the better.'

'I may have a remedy for that,' Esther replied lightly.

'What?' Jack enquired hopefully, but Esther simply replied 'Later', and disappeared into the scullery with two dirty supper plates.

Chapter Eight

'It's beginning to look a lot like an orphanage around here as well.' Constance Enright beamed proudly as she looked out of the sitting room window to where four of her grandchildren were chasing each other up and down the lawn between the rose beds, while the youngest two sat contentedly on their mothers' laps. It was 'full house' for Sunday dinner at the old family home, with her daughter Lucy and husband Teddy also in attendance with their brood, along with Percy and Beattie, and while the cook and housemaid were draped, exhausted, across the kitchen table sharing a pot of tea, the family were resting and sipping their own tea after a magnificent game pie with all the vegetables.

'I just hope I'm feeling up to it when the day comes,' Esther reminded her. 'I got a lot of backache during my other pregnancies, and I'll be around eight months gone by the day of the Spring Fair.'

'I'll obviously be there to assist,' Constance reassured her, 'and there's no shortage of ladies from the Guild who've already volunteered to do the actual baking. Added to which, aren't you planning on roping in a couple of the orphans themselves?'

'Yes, and that reminds me that I'm due to return there to begin their instruction.'

'Who needs any instruction on how to stand behind a table and look pathetic?' Percy chimed in, and when Esther looked outraged, Beattie dug Percy in the ribs to register her displeasure and advised the company that, 'He didn't really mean that. He always gets grumpy when he can't have third helpings.'

'They'll need to do more than stand and look pathetic,' Esther told them all. 'I'm hoping to get them to help with collecting the money, which means I'll have to give them arithmetic training in advance.'

'At the risk of getting another dig in the ribs,' Percy replied, 'make sure that you see the money going into the tin.'

'Percy, that's a *terrible* thing to say!' Beattie chided him. 'Just go outside and set fire to that awful pipe of yours, or something. You can always pretend that you're supervising your great nephews and nieces. That's the only contribution you seem destined to make towards the Enright dynasty.'

'Coming back to the subject of which,' Constance beamed at Esther, 'was Dr Browning able to give you an approximate date for your delivery?'

'Nothing too specific,' Esther replied. 'The nearest he could offer was late August or early September.'

'At least all the birthday parties will be spread well apart,' Constance smiled. 'Miriam in February, Bertie in April, and Lily in July. And now the new arrival in September.'

'Have you booked a midwife yet?' Beattie asked.

Esther shook her head. 'I've not had time, since I only found out on Thursday that I'd be needing one. I'm not sure that Jack's quite recovered from the shock yet.'

'Oh yes I have,' Jack retorted, 'it's just that the case that I'm working on at the moment is all about babies, adoptions and so on.'

'The case *we're* working on,' Percy reminded him. 'And quite the wrong sort of infant care, let me remind you.'

'And let *me* remind you two of our rule against talking about work during Sunday dinner,' Constance admonished them.

'Jackson, I blame you for that lapse, and perhaps Beattie's right that Percy should be encouraged to take his pipe outside."

'I think I'll take up pipe smoking,' Jack muttered as he followed Percy through the sliding doors into the rear garden and yelled to Bertie not to fight with Lily over the use of the swing.

'I wish she'd stop suggesting that giving birth to me was like having her appendix removed without chloroform,' Jack complained as he sat with Esther, Percy and Beattie round the kitchen table after a supper of cauliflower cheese that none of them had really needed after their excessive dinner.

'She's proud of having you, that's all,' Beattie assured him, 'in the same way that your Uncle Percy and I are proud of how you turned out.'

'Uncle Percy might not be when he learns how little progress I've made in this latest case,' Jack replied sadly.

Beattie rose from the table. 'I'll take that as my cue to make myself scarce and read to the children until bedtime. Lily was nodding off before we even left your mother's and I think she'll be in the Land of Nod before I get to the second chapter. Anyway, don't let me keep you from unfolding Percy's game board.'

With Percy's chart spread across the kitchen table, its author related the sad tidings regarding his failure to track down Annabelle Grant. Then he smiled across at Esther. 'However, I wasn't to know at the time that we have in our company a lady who will shortly be in need of infant clothes.'

'I was already ahead of you on that, and the answer's "yes", of course. I've always wanted to dress my babies in really "high class" shawls and matinee coats, and "Timothy's" sounds like a splendid place to buy them.'

'I didn't misunderstand that, did I?' Jack asked. 'We're going to pose as proud parents to be and go and see this "Frances Dickinson" for ourselves?'

'We *are* proud parents to be, I hope,' Esther frowned across at him, 'and I haven't been able to employ my pregnancy to good effect in one of your cases since I visited that abortionist in the West End years ago. So yes — when shall we do it?'

'Next Saturday, I suggest,' Percy told her. 'The store will be at its busiest at that time and she won't have cause to remember you in the future, should we need to employ you in a different capacity. Added to which, Jack and I can claim overtime if we also work on Sunday, following up what we get from the day before.'

'Not to mention avoiding another Sunday dinner at Mother's,' Jack pointed out. 'Perhaps we can take a boat on the Thames and examine the tidal flow at low tide, since all I can add to our store of information is that the latest Essex one probably began its corpse life somewhere in the Docks area.'

'And that would be consistent with something that's occurred to me,' Esther announced proudly.

'She's been bursting with this all week,' Jack explained to Percy with a dismissive smile. 'I don't know what got her more excited — the new baby, or the devastating revelation that she's about to impart.'

'Ignore him, my dear,' Percy advised her. 'Whenever his school lost a cricket match, he always blamed the umpire. So, what have you got for us?'

'Just a thought, that's all. Nothing spectacular,' Esther warned them.

'And?' Percy coaxed her.

'Well, the four East End ones — Shoreditch, Whitechapel, Wapping and Stepney — may have more in common than simply their proximity to each other.'

'Meaning?' Percy prompted her with a hopeful smile.

'Well, look at where the bodies were dumped, probably under cover of darkness. A railway carriage, a printer's workshop, a dockyard and a gutter. Who might be able to access each of those places without drawing attention to themselves?' She looked at both of them in turn, noting the expectant looks on their faces, and eventually decided to answer her own question. 'Prostitutes, that's who. Take the railway carriage, for a start. It's well known that the better class of street totty usually has somewhere more convenient and comfortable to take their client than a back alley, and even I've heard stories of empty railway carriages being put to energetic use after nightfall. Any self-respecting prostitute would know how to pick the lock on a carriage door — if they're even kept locked — and that would explain the Shoreditch one.'

'The printer's workshop in Whitechapel? Jack challenged her.

Esther smiled. 'Again, local totties soon get to know which locks can be picked and which doors are left unlocked in their local neighbourhoods. A girl seen slipping into a darkened workshop yard wouldn't attract much attention, since everyone would assume that she's going in there with a customer.'

'St Katherine Dock sees more action during the hours of darkness than when it's actually being used as a dock, so that fits as well,' Percy conceded. 'But a simple gutter in Stepney?'

'Again, a girl, or woman, alone at night, walking a darkened street, would be taken for a totty and would have all the time in the world, in between gas lamps, to roll something into the gutter from the carpet bag that many heave their worldly goods around in between doss houses.'

'Your intimate knowledge of the East End flesh trade is both impressive and, for me, slightly worrying,' Jack muttered sarcastically.

Esther smiled. 'I lived for some time in a common lodging house in Spitalfields, remember? I saw them come and go, and I heard their conversations when they were sobering up the next morning in the communal kitchen. I could still guide you to favoured locations for sexual encounters and make an educated guess at the going rates for most intimate services, without actually hitching up my own skirts.'

'If you're right,' Percy murmured as his own thought process rumbled into action, 'and these East End infant bodies were dumped by totties, then are you suggesting that the babies were their own — that they were just coincidental and random dumpings — or that someone was controlling the distribution network from a central place in the scheme and simply offering the totties a chance to earn a few extra pence without the need for the usual unpleasantness and personal energy?'

'That's for the real detectives to discover.' Esther smiled. 'I'm just giving you the benefit of my several years surrounded by all that squalor. All you need to do now is interview the several thousand ladies of the night in the East End,' she added sarcastically.

'Terrific,' Jack muttered. 'They'll go nicely with the one I've got to speak to in the morning, who has the bare-faced cheek to accuse a mark of raping her.'

Chapter Nine

It was a very grumpy Jack who looked up as Clara Bristow's arrival was announced by the front desk constable who could barely keep the smirk from his face. Clara flounced into the chair in front of Jack's desk and looked across at him defiantly, then let her eyes drift down to the desk top.

'Shouldn't yer 'ave pencil an' paper ready?'

'You haven't said anything yet,' Jack reminded her with a bored look. 'So, go ahead — amaze me with your capacity for invention.'

'Like I've bin tryin' ter tell youse lot for damn near three weeks, I were raped by Joe Goodman. 'E's the local carrier.'

'When and where?'

'Three Sat'days ago. We 'ad this arrangement that 'e were gonna take me out ter the old mill at Gret Dunmow.'

'Dare I ask what he was to get in return?'

'Whatdyer fink?'

'Yet you claim that he raped you? Was that because he didn't complete his part of the bargain?'

'That's right 'e didn't! We gets ter the windmill, then we 'as this big argument over nuffin', an' 'e threatens ter leave me there on me own, miles from 'ome — *after* 'e's 'ad me, mind you! So I told 'im where 'e could go, an' then 'e starts beltin' me round the 'ead, and then 'e 'ad what 'e wanted, an' just drove off wi'out me. It took me ages ter get 'ome, an' it were dark by then.'

Jack smiled politely. 'This sounds to me more like a breach of contract than rape. However, he had no legal right to hit you around the face and that's all I can do him for, based on what you've told me.'

Clara shot up from her chair, her face contorted in anger. 'Yer all the bloomin' same, you men! Yer treat women like sacks o' potaters, like we've got no feelin's. Then yer stick tergevver when it comes ter sumfink like this. You coppers *never* can believe that a lady can say "no" sometimes, can yer?'

'Sit down, Miss Bristow,' Jack demanded. 'I've already explained that I'm going to charge Joe Goodman with grievous bodily harm or something similar, although a jury might have difficulty even with that, in the circumstances. And I need to know why you wanted to go the abandoned mill in the first place.'

'It were an 'andy place fer the business, weren't it?'

Jack sighed. 'You're taking me around in circles. First you tell me that you agreed to have intercourse with Joe Goodman in exchange for transport to and from the mill, which suggests that you had some other reason for wanting to go there. *Then* you tell me that your reason for wanting to go to the mill was because it was a convenient place to have intercourse with Joe Goodman. That doesn't add up, does it?'

'Well it's the truth.'

'No, it's far from the truth,' Jack persisted. 'Why were you going to the mill in the first place?'

'That's my business,' Clara insisted as she remained standing, but edged nervously towards the door.

'It's also going to have to be mine, if you want Joe Goodman charged with anything,' Jack persevered, now very suspicious that something was being kept from him.

Clara scowled before turning and racing out of Jack's office, clomping down the wooden staircase and swearing and blaspheming at the top of her voice.

A few moments later, Constable Greaves poked his head through the still open doorway and addressed Jack as he sat staring into space, deep in thought.

'You alright, sir? Only the way that totty went steamin' outa here, I thought she might've done yer a mischief.'

'No, but she may have done herself a bit of no good,' Jack replied thoughtfully. 'Pull Joe Goodman in immediately, charged with serious assault, and then bring him up here for questioning.'

Percy sighed as he gazed up at the legend carved in the lintel above the stone entrance to Leman Street Police Station and the memories came flooding back. His first serious work in Whitechapel had been in connection with 'the Ripper' murders seven years previously, although he'd also been back briefly in pursuit of a very evil person who'd been battering people to death during slum clearances in neighbouring Bethnal Green. His previous dealings with 'H' Division had worked out well in the end and perhaps this latest 'needle in a haystack' enquiry would bear fruit, although he doubted it. It was his third police station since he'd started his working day and the others had responded to his request with polite amusement.

After announcing his rank and the nature of his business he was escorted up two flights of stairs to the office of Inspector Gladwell, an eager looking man whose relative youth for such a rank was belied by his almost total lack of hair. His 'chrome dome' shone under the gas light as he invited Percy to explain his business.

Percy coughed with embarrassment as he began. 'You recently had a dead baby dumped in the yard of "Bentley Printworks" in Chamber Street, plus one fished out of St Katherine's Dock in Wapping. I assume you're treating them as murder cases and I was wondering if there was any progress to report.'

Gladwell frowned. 'No, and if there had been you'd have received the usual circular by wire at the Yard, so why are you *really* here, Inspector?'

Percy's hopes rose. Not only was this man nobody's fool, but he might even be capable of grasping the enormity of his enquiry. 'The fact is,' he replied conspiratorially, 'that you weren't the only police division to get one during a fairly short period of time and we think there may be a connection between all four, of which one of yours was a "double event" with one dumped in a gutter in Stepney on the same night.'

'I seem to remember reading the wire on the Stepney one,' Gladwell confirmed, 'but how do you think they may be connected, and have you spoken to Stepney about it?'

'I've just come from there,' Percy replied with a grimace, 'and they all but showed me the door.'

'And you think I may have a different attitude?'

'Depends how easily and quickly you want to close your books on two infanticides.' Percy smiled encouragingly.

'So how can I help?'

'We — by which I mean my associates at the Yard and myself — believe that the person who dumped the babies in both cases may have been a street prostitute, and possibly the same one.'

'Someone who recently gave birth to twins in a sordid back room somewhere, you mean?'

'That might be one possibility, certainly,' Percy conceded, 'but an alternative theory might be that the "lady" in question was paid to dump them, making use of her ability to navigate the dark places that make up the East End at night.'

'Paid by whom?'

'If I knew that, I wouldn't be taking up your valuable time,' Percy told him, wondering if the man was so bright after all. 'That's where I require your assistance.'

'Would you care to be more specific?'

'Well, you're pulling these girls off the streets every night, are you not? Some of them are inclined to make a trade for their freedom — and I don't just mean on their backs in an empty cell, and don't pretend it doesn't happen, because I know differently.'

'So?'

'So, I'm prepared to put the backing of the Yard behind you if you lose the charge against any girl who can give you reliable information regarding the dumping of dead babies. Either who's been doing it, or who's offering money to the girls for doing it. I've left the same offer with not only Stepney, but also the Commercial Road lot in Shoreditch, who fished one out of a parked railway carriage.'

'That certainly sounds promising,' Gladwell smirked. 'I only hope the girls clean up those carriages after they've used them.'

'But you get the point?' Percy urged him. 'Hold the charge once you hear something that you think might be of interest to me, then wire me at the Yard and I'll come down and conduct a more detailed interview with the lady in question.'

'Of course,' Gladwell assured him, 'but we sometimes pull in twenty totties a night down here. It's going to cause a traffic jam in the fish tank until we can haul each of them into an interview room separately and enquire about dead babies of their acquaintance.'

'I hope I'm not hearing "it's all too hard",' Percy grumbled with a warning in his voice.

'No, of course not — just pointing out the problems it'll create. So how long do you want us to keep this up for?'

'As long as it takes,' Percy advised him. 'Starting tonight and going on forever, until we get a result. Now, is that pie shop still open for business on the corner out there?'

'I ain't done nuffin', so what's this all about?' Joe Goodman complained as he loomed above Jack's desk, a picture of moral outrage. Jack assessed his bulk and instructed Constable Greaves to remain in the doorway, while inviting Goodman to take a seat.

'I recently had the dubious pleasure of viewing the extensive bruises on Clara Bristow's face,' Jack told him, 'and she advises me that you were the one responsible for them.'

'She's a stupid tart,' Goodman objected.

Jack smiled unpleasantly. 'At least we can agree on one thing, Mr Goodman, but there seems to be some disagreement between us regarding how she came by her bruises. Do you at least concede that you and she came to an agreement three Saturdays ago that you'd transport her on your cart to an abandoned windmill at Great Dunmow, in return for enjoying her favours?'

'Yeah, so what? She's a totty, an' I'm not married, so what's yer problem?'

'My problem, Mr Goodman, is that according to her not only did you not keep your end of the bargain, in the sense that you failed to carry her home as agreed, but you also inflicted severe facial bruising on her, then had your way with her.'

'Wiv 'er consent, let me remind yer,' Goodman growled.

Jack smiled again. 'I don't propose to embark on a lecture on the laws of contract, Mr Goodman, nor am I particularly concerned about whether or not you enjoyed her favours under false pretences. But as even you must appreciate, you can't go around using a woman's face as some sort of training punch bag.'

'She asked forrit,' Goodman growled again, his face now pointing down at the desk, unable to look Jack in the eye.

'In the sense that she requested a severe belting?' Jack said with heavy sarcasm.

'No, obviously not,' Goodman conceded. 'It were what she were doin' up there in the first place. I objected, an' she told me ter mind me own business, an' I lost it wi' 'er.'

'You're implying that she wasn't up at the mill simply to have sexual relations with you?'

'No, course not. That wouldn't make sense, would it? She wanted ter go ter the mill ter drop off a parcel. It were when I saw what were in the parcel that I lost it wi' er, 'cos she were makin' me a party to 'er crime.'

'Crime?' Jack enquired encouragingly.

Goodman shook his head. 'I'm sayin' nowt more, in case I get done forrit an' all.'

'Done for what?' Jack demanded, but Goodman continued to shake his head, and a different approach was now clearly called for, so Jack cleared his throat and began. 'Let me remind you that at present I'm considering charging you with causing grievous bodily harm, Mr Goodman, or perhaps attempted murder. While a hanging is probably out of the question, given what may have been provocation on Miss Bristow's part, I wouldn't rule out a double figure sentence somewhere very inhospitable, probably with hard labour thrown in for bad measure. On the other hand…'

'What yer wantin' ter know?' Goodman said suspiciously.

'What was in that parcel that so incensed you at the time.'

'I don't wanner go down fer murder.'

'You won't, let me assure you,' Jack replied eagerly as his heart began racing harder, 'if you confirm what I already suspect. There was a dead body in that parcel wasn't there?'

'Yeah,' Goodman nodded reluctantly.

'And you agree that it was only a "parcel". So, it was a small body?'

'I won't go ter jail — for owt?' Goodman said anxiously.

Jack shook his head. 'Not if you answer this final question honestly. Was it a baby's body?'

'Yeah,' Goodman confirmed as his voice began to crack with uncharacteristic emotion. 'Just a wee bubby, it were. Not more than a few weeks old, I reckon. It were 'orrible.'

Jack looked up at Constable Greaves. 'Mr Goodman is free to leave later today, with no charge against him. But before that, place him in the best cell we've got and make sure that he's fed while he's our guest.'

'Yer promised me there'd be no charges!' Goodman thundered.

'And there won't be, Mr Goodman, let me assure you. But I don't want you tipping off Miss Bristow before I've sent constables out to Great Dunmow to find the parcel containing the dead baby and had the lady who put it there brought in on a murder charge.'

Chapter Ten

'Hello again,' Percy called over the front gate to where Emily Talbot was pruning her rose brushes in the early afternoon sun. 'Am I too early for tea and crumpets?'

'It'll have to be tea and ginger cake, I'm afraid,' Miss Talbot told him with a broad smile, 'but do come in, and don't mind Barney.'

Percy passed down the side of the house in time to assist Miss Talbot in erecting the shade under which the tea table sat, then take the tea tray from her when she emerged from her kitchen door.

'Have you decided to take up bridge, or do you have more questions for me?' Miss Talbot asked. 'If it's the latter, then I rather fear that I told you all I can regarding the goings on next door.'

'Not quite, perhaps,' Percy corrected her gently. 'There was a period towards the end there — while Miss Grant was still running her adoption agency — when the people coming and going next door weren't quite what you'd call "top drawer", wasn't there?'

'You've been talking to the Boothroyds, haven't you?' Miss Talbot said guardedly. 'Is it true that the girl who lives in their house — the girl called "Sarah" — was acquired from Miss Grant's agency?'

'I'm like you, Miss Talbot,' Percy replied, smiling, as he selected another slice of ginger cake, 'I'm not one for gossip, and I didn't see any girl when I called in there. However, Mr Boothroyd did tell me that towards the end of Miss Grant's tenancy you made frequent complaints regarding the activities next door at Number Seventeen.'

Miss Talbot frowned. 'Alfred Boothroyd was too full of his own self-importance to want to soil his hands with complaints from a "fussy old nosey parker", as he once called me. Can you imagine that?'

Percy just stopped himself in time from nodding his agreement, and instead looked enquiringly over the top of his third slice of cake in the hope that she'd keep going. She duly obliged.

'I wrote letter after letter complaining about the "low types" who kept coming and going, and he and his other self-appointed local pomposities who had the nerve to call themselves a residents' association just ignored my complaints. In the end I notified the police that I thought the place had become a — well, a "house of assignation", if you get my meaning.'

'Yes, indeed I do,' Percy confirmed, 'and I can of course check with them, but perhaps you can relieve me of that burden by telling me what action they took.'

Miss Talbot snorted and shook her head. 'Absolutely nothing, so far as I could tell, although Miss Grant did give up her tenancy very shortly after that — no more than a couple of weeks as I recall. Then that dreadful bookie and his harpy of a wife moved in. At least, one had to assume that she was his wife, although I kept myself very much to myself after that.'

'You didn't mention anything about Miss Grant's unsuitable visitors during our last conversation, Miss Talbot.'

'No, well, like I said, I'm not one for gossip, and I could have been wrong. In fact, when the police did nothing and advised me by letter that they'd investigated my complaint and discovered nothing untoward, I felt rather guilty and ashamed of my behaviour. I was probably just being an old snob, and who wants to listen to the nervous drivel of an elderly spinster?'

'I do, on this occasion,' Percy replied with a warm encouraging smile. 'Tell me what you remember.'

'Well, the women who took to visiting, for a start. More like young girls, some of them, and all very loud and — well, "tarty" is the only word I could honestly employ. They all wore cheap clothing — you know, bright colours, ridiculous hats, skirts up to their ankles — and they were always laughing and shouting to each other. There was always more than one in each coach, and they were carrying overnight bags as they came and went, so you can quite understand why I thought that the place was turning into a — a "bordello" I believe is the word.'

'Did they appear to be lodging there overnight?' Percy asked, hoping for a negative response.

'I didn't pay that much attention, dear, to tell you the truth. I just hid behind my front lace curtains and blushed sometimes at what they were shouting to each other, all about how much money they'd be earning, and where they were heading for.'

'Do you by any chance remember any of the places they mentioned?' Percy prompted her.

'I remember a reference to the Docks, because one of the loudest of the girls squawked something along the lines of 'This is for the docks,' or something like that, and I seem to recall mention of some of those dreadful places in London that one reads about. You know — where those horrible murders were committed.'

'Whitechapel?'

'That's the place. And is there somewhere in the same area called "Bethleham Green"? I remember hearing two of the girls arranging to meet up there the following evening.'

Percy tried not to laugh as he advised her that she'd probably heard the name 'Bethnal Green' and rose politely to leave.

'There are some really nice people living next door now,' Miss Talbot told him. 'He's an artist, and she teaches piano in her front room. Would you like me to take you over and introduce you?'

Assuring her that he appreciated the offer, but had to return to his duties, Percy left for the front gate with a broad smile on his face, broken only when he turned to give Barney a friendly growl on his way down the front path. Noting that the sun was beginning to sink, he quickened his pace, and arrived breathlessly at the property office he'd visited only the previous week.

The same man — Lionel Winters — was behind the counter, and he smiled instinctively as Percy walked towards his counter.

'I recall you, of course,' Winters assured Percy. 'Didn't you buy the Arthur place?'

'No,' Percy sighed with irritation, 'I'm the police officer who was here last week, enquiring about Seventeen Cedar Lane, and giving you free advice on how you might improve your vetting procedures.'

'Ah, yes,' Winters recalled through his disappearing smile. 'How can I help you further?'

'Aren't you assuming that you were of assistance *last* time?' Percy replied acidly. 'But presumably even your sparse and inaccurate records can reveal if Miss Grant vacated the property at the natural termination of her lease, or a little earlier than previously scheduled.'

Winters pulled out the file, adjusted his glasses and squinted into the paperwork. 'Difficult to tell, to be honest. The rent was certainly paid up until the end of the term, and we were rather hoping that she'd exercise the late option to renew, but then we learned that she'd simply upped and left with several weeks still to run. That worked out well for us, of course, because we were then able to find new tenants while we had vacant possession, although they turned out to be less than satisfactory.'

'Any idea why Miss Grant closed up shop and left so abruptly?'

'No, although it might have been you lot making enquiries. A rather juvenile constable came in here a couple of times, asking if Miss Grant was a desirable tenant, and if we'd had any complaints or suspicions about her running a brothel, which of course we denied.'

'I rather gain the impression that even if Miss Grant had been organising an armed military uprising down there, you'd have had no idea, and even less concern, provided that the rent was paid on time,' Percy remarked sourly, 'but may I take it that Miss Grant left somewhat hastily?'

'I suppose you could draw that conclusion,' Winters conceded. 'The new people are excellent tenants, I might add.'

'So their busybody neighbour told me,' Percy replied. 'Perhaps you should have consulted her from the start — it might have saved you the expense of repairing the drains. Before I leave, hopefully for the final time, you might wish to hand over one of those bogus references that were supplied to you by Miss Grant. For all the use you made of them then, you can hardly claim that you need them now.'

'You were right, sir,' Detective Constable Billy Manvers advised Jack as he rushed into his office without knocking. 'We found an infant corpse in a cardboard box under the mill wheel. It's pretty far gone, but if you ask me it was only a few weeks old.'

'I think we'll leave the determination of age to the police surgeon, Constable,' Jack replied. 'You might want to concentrate instead on bringing in Miss Bristow.'

'Already done, sir. She's down in the cells, shouting like a fishmonger on market day about the injustices of life, and the incompetence and corruption of the police.'

'Good work, Billy. Tell her that when she's calmed down and considered her position she can come up here for an unbiased conversation about how she happened to be in possession of a dead baby in a box.'

Jack had to wait for over half an hour before a dishevelled and aggrieved looking Clara Bristow was led into his office, attached to Detective Constable Manvers by a set of handcuffs.

'I'll take them off if you promise to behave yourself,' Manvers advised her, and when she nodded, he slipped off the cuffs and stood resolutely in the open doorway, just in case. Jack motioned her into a chair and she looked across his desk with a pleading expression.

'I didn't murder that bubby — 'onest I didn't!'

'Well, that's what you'll be charged with until you tell me who did,' Jack informed her, then sat back with a pencil poised over a notepad.

Clara looked him squarely in the eyes and began to relate her life's history.

'I were born in a village called Stebling Ford, near Braintree, an' I were the youngest o' three sisters. The other two were right pretty, an' got theirselves married pretty young, leavin' me on the shelf. It were just me an me Mam in them days, an' we was tight fer money, so she took in a lodger what worked on a farm down the road. It were obvious that 'im an' me Mam were at it, then she went an' died, an' 'e transferred 'is affections ter me. Then 'e buggered off when sumfink better crossed 'is path, leavin' me in a right mess wi' a bubby on the way.'

'A familiar enough tale,' Jack nodded sympathetically, 'but where is it taking us?'

Clara snorted, then replied.

'I'm gettin' ter that, if yer gimme the chance. The fact is I couldn't keep the bubby, on account that I were plannin' on doin' livin' in work at the big 'ouse up the road what were owned by this fancy lawyer from London. Then I were told about this woman called Martha Bradley what lived down in Little Waltham, an' could find 'omes fer bubbies whose muvvers couldn't keep 'em. So I went an' saw 'er, an' give 'er five shillin's, what was me life savin's, an' she took the bub when it were only a few weeks old. A girl, it were.'

'And?' Jack demanded impatiently.

'Well,' Clara continued, 'a few weeks back Martha Bradley come ter see me. She told me that me bubby 'ad died, an' that it were all my fault, an' if she told the bobbies I'd be 'ung. Then she promised me she'd say nowt if I did this little favour for 'er, 'cos she'd got another coupla bubbies what 'ad died, only she need someone ter get rid o' their little bodies. So I agreed.'

'Not just the one in the mill, then?' Jack asked, all ears.

'No — there was three altogevver. But I didn't kill 'em meself, 'onest I didn't.'

'Think carefully,' Jack demanded. 'Where did you put the other two?'

'Easy ter remember, 'cos it were 'orrible, an' I didn't think I 'ad any choice in the matter. The first un went under some bales o' hay in a cow barn out Riven'all way, then I put the second in a bin out the back've a pub in Harlow, where a gentleman friend an' me 'ad gone fer an evenin's refreshment. I took it in me bag, then made out that I needed ter powder me nose an' slipped outside wi' it.'

'And what about the one in the Thames near West Mersea?'

'Don't know nowt about that, 'onest I don't. It were just the three, like I said.'

'This "Martha Bradbury" — would you be able to identify her for us if we brought her in?'

'O' course, but I don't want no trouble fer meself. I didn't murder no bubbies, not even me own, an' that's the 'onest truth.'

'Did you ever go to Martha Bradbury's house?'

'No, never. She come ter me wi' the three dead bubbies what needed ter be 'idden. One've 'em — the one what went in the barn — were little more than a skellington, by the way.'

'But how did you contact this woman in the first place?' Jack pressed her. 'Surely you must have gone to her house that first time — when you handed your child over?'

'No,' Clara insisted with a firm shake of her head. 'I were told she could always be found in "The Wheatsheaf" in Little Waltham, an' that's where I met up wi' 'er. She come ter me ter collect me bub, an' that's when I give 'er the five shillin's.'

'So when did you last see her?'

'A month or so back, when she give me the bubs ter get rid o', like I said.'

'And she didn't say why she couldn't get rid of them herself?'

'No, but I reckon it were because she were too respectable lookin' ter get away wi' it. A woman like me you'd expect ter see 'angin' round farmers' sheds, empty mills an' pub yards. But not a woman like 'er.'

'But not too respectable to be seen in "The Wheatsheaf" in Little Waltham?'

'It were the "snug" bar where I met 'er, an' I got some funny looks from the barmaid, like I didn't belong in there. But when I enquired fer Martha Bradbury, the snooty cow nodded ter the women in the corner, an' after that there were no suggestion o' chuckin' me out.'

'So what did she look like?

Clara thought for a moment before replying. 'Quite short, wi' dark 'air cut close ter 'er 'ead, like she were a nun or sumfink. Thin face, an' I think she 'ad kinda black eyes. Leastways, they seemed black when they was pointin' at yer.'

Jack stared at the ceiling before nodding to Billy Manvers. 'This young lady's free to go for the time being. The only charge might be interfering with a corpse, but we'll decide that later, and you'll definitely be hearing from us again sooner or later, Miss Bristow. In the meantime, behave yourself, no more disposals of dead babies, and keep quiet about what you've told us this morning.'

'What about the charges against Joe Goodman?'

'Don't push your luck, Miss Bristow,' Jack said, smiling, as she was escorted out. A few moments later Billy Manvers reappeared in Jack's doorway.

'She's on her way rejoicing, sir. Do you want me to check out "The Wheatsheaf", to see if we can locate this Martha Bradbury?'

'No, you can leave that to me, Constable. In the meantime, I have to commandeer one of the police coaches for a trip to Brentwood.'

Esther smiled encouragingly at Nell and Billy as they sat, eager-faced, in front of her in the small classroom in the orphanage that they'd been allowed the use of for an hour. They'd been joined by Margaret Meacher, who'd taken a break from helping to supervise the Senior Girls' sewing class, and they were hoping to create efficient sales persons out of the two young people who'd be helping out at the cake stall at St Margaret's Summer Fair.

'Now then,' Esther coaxed them, 'suppose I sell three cakes at tuppence each, and the lady buying them gives me a shilling, how much change would I need to give her?'

It went silent for a moment, until Billy asked, 'What kind o' cakes, Miss?'

'It doesn't matter what kind of cakes, does it?' Esther replied. 'Just concentrate on the money.'

'Twelve pence less six pence,' Margaret offered by way of assistance.

Billy still looked blank until Nell whispered in his ear, then he grinned. 'Sixpence, Miss. You'd need to give the lady back sixpence.'

'You knew, didn't you?' Esther grinned at Nell with a sly conspiratorial expression. 'You knew, and you told Billy, didn't you?'

'I didn't want him to look ignorant, Miss,' was Nell's justification.

Esther chuckled. 'I sometimes perform a similar service for my husband, but these men have to learn to fend for themselves, so this time don't help him. I'll try to make it easy. Now then…'

Half an hour later, Billy was beginning to get the hang of simple numbers when applied to the selling of cakes, while Nell clearly needed no further instruction. Then a young nun appeared in the open classroom doorway and smiled at Esther.

'There's a gentleman at the front door who says he's your husband, madam.'

Esther turned to Billy and Nell. 'It's probably close to your dinner time, so well done — both of you — and I'll come back in a week or two and see how much you remember. Now I think that my husband wishes to take me to dinner here in town, so off you go.'

The two of them scampered off down the corridor towards the dining room, and Esther turned to Margaret with a smile. 'I think we'll get there in the end. Nell's obviously brighter than Billy, but she's determined to help him along. Quite sweet, really.'

'In my experience it's the girls who learn quicker than the boys,' Margaret replied. 'Not that I had any of my own, of course, but being associated for so long with the children here I've come to notice that.'

'Would you like to meet my husband Jack?' Esther asked. 'He's very kindly agreed to collect me and take me to dinner, since he knows how I hate those bus trips — particularly those bumpy roads, in my condition — and the train times just aren't very convenient.'

'I'd be delighted,' Margaret beamed, 'since I've never really met a proper detective before.'

'You'll find that he's more of an overgrown schoolboy, but I love him dearly,' Esther told her. 'Perhaps you'd care to join us for dinner?'

'Only if you let me pay; there's a very nice bakery just down the road here that has tables out at the front, and they make lovely chicken pies. It's a warm enough day, so we can sit out on the pavement.'

'That was my very first trip in a police coach,' Margaret said a few minutes later as they sat enjoying the midday sun at a table outside the 'Baker's Delight' and savouring a chicken pie each.

'We have to hope that it's your last,' Jack replied, smiling, 'since we normally use them for transporting criminals.'

'I certainly have no ambition to fall into that category!' Margaret assured him. 'Will that nice young coachman get some dinner as well?'

'He will if there's a pub down the road there.' Jack nodded down the street in the direction in which the coachman had driven off. 'Let's hope that he's still sober when the time comes to drive us all the way back to Barking.'

'You managed to get the rest of the day off then, like you promised?' Esther asked.

Jack nodded. 'One of the big advantages of being your own boss, and I had quite a productive morning. Which reminds me, Margaret — Esther told me that you began your association with the orphanage when you brought a few waifs and strays into their protection.'

'That's correct,' Margaret affirmed. 'There was a lady living locally in Braintree — or at least, she always used our Post Office, so I assumed that she was local — and she spent her time and money caring for children who would otherwise have finished up in the gutter, or worse. We got talking and when I mentioned my admiration for the work of orphanages, she advised me of the existence of the Holy Heart here in Brentwood and asked if I would approach them to take in the occasional child she'd been looking after.'

'Was she by any chance small, with short-cropped dark hair and intense dark eyes?'

'Yes — how did you know?'

'Calling herself Martha Bradbury?'

'No — her name was Harriet Merchant.'

'Are you still in contact with her?'

'No. There came a time when the orphanage couldn't take any more of her children. Then she stopped coming to our shop, and I assumed that she'd moved to another area.'

'She did, I'm afraid,' Jack advised her, 'Little Waltham.'

'Why did you say "afraid" just then?' Margaret said in a quavering voice, as Esther sat silently with a horrified expression on her face.

Jack coughed nervously as he replied. 'I can't say too much, but I'd be very keen to catch up with your Harriet Merchant and my Martha Bradbury.'

'Why is that?' Margaret persisted, and despite Esther's vigorous head shake in his direction Jack decided that this worthy lady deserved an explanation.

'Because my Martha Bradbury's still supplying babies, Mrs Meacher. But they're dead ones.'

'That was *so* embarrassing,' Esther hissed at Jack as the coach rumbled back in the direction of Barking, leaving Margaret Meacher on the pavement outside the bakery, still dabbing the handkerchief to her eyes. 'Couldn't you see me warning you to shut your silly mouth? I sort of guessed what was coming, and Margaret Meacher's too nice a person to deserve that. Sometimes you have the sensitivity of a rampaging bull!'

'I was only doing my job, and it's not the sort of work that calls for shrinking violets,' Jack explained. 'You didn't give me time to explain before you introduced me to your orphanage colleague, but this morning I identified the person who dumped three infant bodies around the county. The third one isn't even on our list yet, since I only found out about it a few days ago. But she confessed to dumping two of the original three, and it's probably the case that the one in the Thames just drifted down from further up.'

'This was that Martha Bradbury who you ruined Margaret's dinner by mentioning?'

'Yes and no,' Jack replied. The actual dumping in that farmer's shed in Rivenhall and the pub yard in Harlow was done by a local prostitute, who also slipped one under the wheel of an abandoned mill in Great Dunmow. But she was put up to it by a woman calling herself, at that time, "Martha Bradbury", although to your friend Margaret she was also known as "Harriet Merchant". And I think that she may be found in a pub called "The Wheatsheaf" in Little Waltham.'

'Is that where we're going now?' Esther asked with a concerned frown. 'Only I told your mother I'd be home by four o'clock.'

'We'll both be home long before then,' Jack reassured her as he extracted his fob watch and consulted it. 'I've made enough progress for one day, and as for you, remember that we have a date with Uncle Percy to go shopping for baby clothes on Saturday.'

'Even *that* little outing's to do with a police investigation,' Esther complained. 'When we first met, we'd hold hands on Sunday afternoons and walk through that churchyard, and dream about what might be ahead of us. Now it's behind us, and we only hold hands when we're posing as a normal husband and wife for the benefit of another of your Uncle Percy's devious schemes for unmasking criminals.'

'Only because you volunteer for that sort of thing so eagerly,' Jack reminded her. 'Just say the word if you want to give it up and lead a quiet life.'

'Life married to you could never be "quiet", Jack Enright,' Esther said, smiling, as she leaned sideways to kiss his cheek. 'As for giving it all up, forget it. *Someone* has to protect you from yourself.'

Chapter Eleven

Jack sighed with frustration as he cast his eyes sightlessly over the mass of paper on his desk, the result of several days of intense enquiry through the criminal records held by not only Scotland Yard, but also the forces in outlying counties such as Essex, Middlesex, Surrey, Kent and Hertfordshire. They had plenty of 'Martha Bradburys' on record, and quite a few 'Harriet Merchant' entries, but none of them quite matched the profile of a woman who was likely to have been responsible for the cold-blooded murder of an unknown number of innocent babies. He'd unearthed countless thieves, a blackmailer, and a fraudster, plus a woman with a lengthy record for prostitution and brothel-keeping. His hopes had risen at that point, only to be dashed when he read the report more carefully and discovered that the lady in question had died in prison in 1887.

It didn't make it any easier that the woman changed her name so often. Was she the same person as 'Annabelle Grant' from Surrey, who was allegedly now calling herself 'Frances Dickinson'? Or were there even more aliases that they would unearth before this woman was eventually tracked down and buckled? Alternatively, were they dealing with more than one organiser? With nothing better to do, he began doodling the names on a spare piece of paper in front of him. Then a thought struck him, and he fired off yet another round of requests for criminal histories, using variations of the same names in different combinations. This time he was enquiring into the criminal histories of women calling themselves 'Frances Grant', 'Annabelle Merchant', and 'Harriet Bradbury'. He'd make himself about as popular as a dose of the pox in the process, but nobody could accuse him of not being thorough and he just hoped that the same idea hadn't occurred to Uncle Percy, else the result would be an unjustified waste of manpower.

He might as well try the obvious, he decided with reluctance. He couldn't claim to have done a proper job without making at least an attempt to enquire about a 'Martha Bradbury' at The Wheatsheaf in Little Waltham. If that failed, he'd try her alias of 'Harriet Merchant', but in both cases he fully anticipated that he'd be met with stern-faced denials by pub employees who'd been well bribed. At least it was Thursday, and not the customary Friday pay day, when the pub would be heaving with drunks investing the family's food money for the following week.

The result was precisely as he expected. Avoiding the public bar, he walked through to the better class 'snug', which was almost empty apart from two shamefaced elderly ladies, both of whom looked embarrassed to be found in there, but neither of whom even vaguely fitted the image of child murderers. The slovenly woman behind the bar, who no doubt believed that she could still be described as a 'girl', looked back blankly at him as he ordered a half pint of best bitter.

'You a copper?' she demanded accusingly.

'Do I look like a copper?' Jack replied.

'Yeah, yer do — else I wouldn't be askin', would I?'

'Actually, I'm hoping to meet Martha Bradbury in here.'

'Yer'll wait a long time then, 'cos we ain't seen 'er in months. So if yer *are* a copper, an' yer find 'er, yer might care ter remind 'er that she still owes us five bob.'

'How about Harriet Merchant?'

'Who?'

'Never mind.'

He finished his half pint and moved towards the door. As he did so, one of the elderly ladies looked up from her drink and waved him over.

'You were asking about someone called "Harriet Merchant", that right?'

'Yes — do you know her?'

'I might have done. Did she live in Braintree at one time?'

'Possibly,' Jack replied, 'but I heard that she'd moved out here to Little Waltham.'

'I sincerely hope not, after the trouble she caused in Braintree when I lived next door to her.'

'What sort of trouble?'

'Well, not so much trouble as noise. Screaming kids. She never seemed to have a man around the place, but there was no shortage of babies. The funny thing was, in the three years or so that she lived next door, the babies never seemed to grow up — or grow out of the screaming stage. A proper nuisance, it was.'

'Clarissa,' the woman behind the bar shouted across the room, 'if you was 'opin' ter be served wi' another drink in 'ere, that's enough gossip. Particularly when it's wi' a copper.'

'I'll remember your co-operation when the time comes for your licence renewal,' Jack said sardonically before thanking the old lady and kicking the swing door open on his way out.

'This must be the place,' Jack announced as he looked up at the sign above the door of the busy cafe in Oxford Street. 'Uncle Percy knows every eating place in London, I reckon, and I'd bet money on his having been here for an hour already, eating meat pies in the course of duty.'

'Just don't expect me to eat one,' Esther muttered grumpily. 'In my condition everything I eat makes me want to throw up, and that horrible train journey in from Barking, not to mention that smelly, bumpy horse bus down from Fenchurch Street, did nothing to help, believe me.'

'You've just gone soft with all that country living,' Jack assured her. 'Think yourself lucky you don't have my train journey in each direction every day. Ah, as I suspected, there he is — hidden behind the meat pie collection.'

Percy was seated in a corner booth, grinning to himself as he watched Jack and Esther searching for him. He rose from his seat out of politeness towards Esther and asked if they would like a meat pie.

'No thanks — and neither would Jack,' Esther replied with a commanding air. 'God alone knows what they put in those things, but these days, as a responsible wife and mother, I know the value of good, wholesome, nutritious meals. So, finish yours and we can get on with it.'

'You're beginning to sound like Mother,' Jack complained, 'and Percy and I need to catch up before we go blundering in there.'

'Hurry up, then,' Esther conceded as she slid into the bench opposite Percy's in the booth.

'So?' Jack asked Percy, who shook his head.

'Nothing really beyond what we suspected already. The property in Cobham was almost certainly being used as some sort of clearing house from which girls were coming in from the city to collect babies for disposal. The lady in charge was calling herself "Annabelle Grant", as I already mentioned, and hopefully you'll be meeting her inside the department store in her manifestation as "Frances Dickinson", although all we have to go on is the description. "Fair hair going grey, quite tall, big bosom and a squint in one eye." Do you think you'll be able to spot her with that information? What have you got, Jack?'

Jack smiled. 'I know who dumped the babies in Essex — at least, all but the one in the Thames, which is probably one of yours. It was that totty I mentioned last Sunday. She was almost certainly supplied with them by a lady calling herself either "Martha Bradley" or "Harriet Merchant". I've pulled all the criminal histories under those names and got nowhere. So I tried mixing all the first and second names into different combinations — including your Annabelle Grant — and some of their criminal histories began arriving late yesterday. I've taken them home to look at tomorrow, by which time I'll be able to give you the results of our little expedition today.'

'Beattie and I will be over at around three o'clock,' Percy told them, 'and I only hope that your mother never finds out that we ducked Sunday dinner with her.'

Twenty minutes later Jack and Esther found themselves at the "Mother and Toddler" displays inside the "Infants and Children" section on the ground floor of Timothy's down the road in Oxford Street. They made their way towards the main sales counter, where a rosy cheeked girl of no more than eighteen years of age beamed back at them.

'Good day, sir — madam. What can I assist you with?'

'We're expecting a baby in September and we're looking for some suitable clothing for a new born infant,' Jack replied.

'Is it your first?' the girl asked.

'No,' Jack replied, at exactly the same time as Esther said 'Yes'. The girl looked at them with an amused expression before Jack recovered himself explained, 'There was this girl where I used to live, and…'

'Yes, well, enough about that,' Esther cut back in. 'It's *my* first, and that's all that matters to me. We were specially recommended to shop here, and to ask for a Miss Dickinson.'

'One moment, please,' the girl replied, the faint smirk still on her face as she turned away and ducked inside a curtain to the rear of the space behind the counter. She could be heard whispering a few words to someone and was followed out into the counter area by a woman who fitted exactly the description that Percy had supplied.

'I believe you were asking for me?' the lady asked as she looked them over with the one eye that was pointing in their direction. 'I'm Frances Dickinson.'

Another name I need to pass through criminal records, Jack reminded himself as Esther opened up with a fair impersonation of a first-time mother.

'Yes, you were especially recommended by one of my friends from my bridge club,' she enthused. 'This is my first, you see, and I'm not sure how to go about selecting baby garments. I'm told that they grow very quickly, so one shouldn't spend too much on their first clothes, but I'm so excited that I just want to get the best, and I can't wait to see my lovely baby snuggling in the best that money can buy.'

Frances Dickinson smiled. 'I hear that from a lot of ladies in your very blessed position, but if you'll take my advice you'll go for durability rather than appearance. And it's not necessarily the most expensive garment that's the most durable. If you'd care to step this way, I can show you the most appropriate purchases, whether your child turns out to be a girl or a boy. I take it that you don't currently have an account with us?'

'No,' Esther replied as she allowed her face to fall. 'Is that likely to be a problem?'

'No, no, of course not,' Frances purred. 'I'll just need to take some details from you if you're not paying in cash, but that will be largely a formality, I'm sure. Is your husband in employment?'

'Yes, he is,' Jack chimed in, uncomfortable at being referred to in the third person. 'And very gainful employment at that.'

'Quite,' Frances responded dismissively as she all but turned her back on him in the process of leading Esther gently by the arm towards the first of the display stands, leaving Jack to trail along behind them and make a mental note of everything the woman said, as well as embedding her physical appearance into his memory.

Almost thirty minutes later, Esther had selected an impressive quantity of baby clothing, which was in the process of being carefully wrapped by the young girl they'd first spoken to, before Esther could change her mind about any of it.

'I take it that a cheque will suffice?' Jack asked.

Frances nodded. 'If you could write your home address on the reverse of the cheque, along with details of your employer, that will be sufficient.'

'But I could be anyone,' Jack reminded her. 'How do you know that what I write will be the truth, and that we won't just be walking out of here with all this baby clothing after pulling off a massive fraud?'

Frances Dickinson smiled. 'When you've been in this business as long as I have, you pride yourself on being a good judge of character, and I have no reason to doubt your honesty, sir. As for madam, have you yet organised for a nursing home and midwife in anticipation of the happy event?'

'I'm not due until September,' Esther replied in her best naive voice. 'Do you think I should? I was thinking of having the child at home.'

'Where do you live?' Frances asked.

'Clerkenwell,' Esther replied, before Jack could say something inappropriate.

'On the north side,' Frances mused out loud. 'Perhaps you might want to consider entering a nursing home that specialises in child delivery, with all the necessary midwifery services. It's advisable, for your first at least. It just so happens that my cousin — who's a qualified midwife — has just opened a very exclusive and luxuriously equipped nursing home in Highgate, which is of course a very desirable area of town, and is only a short coach journey away from where you live. I happen to have one of her business cards available — would you like one for possible future reference?'

'Yes please!' Esther gushed.

'You enjoyed every minute of that, didn't you?' Jack demanded grumpily as they stood back on the pavement in Oxford Street, carrying several packages under their arms. 'It's a good job they don't charge extra for luggage on the buses.'

'It's bad enough that they charge anything at all for the privilege of being exposed to everyone else's diseases,' Esther replied with a frown, 'not to mention their body odours. I don't suppose we could run to a coach back to the station?'

'Not after the amount *you* spent,' Jack replied. 'But hopefully it will have been worth it. Your next performance as an expectant mother will be at a certain nursing home in Highgate, where I suspect that you can leave your baby behind if you don't want it, but somebody else does. I can only hope that in due course Aunt Beattie is as good at this sort of thing as you are.'

'Why Aunt Beattie?'

'I'll bet you a week's washing up that Uncle Percy decides to pose as a middle-aged man desperate to adopt a child, and to do that convincingly he'll need a woman in tow, and you look far too young and fertile.'

'She won't agree, surely?' Esther objected.

Jack burst out laughing.

'What's so funny?' Esther asked, and by the time that Jack managed a reply he had tears of laughter rolling down his face.

'If Beattie won't agree, he might be tempted to ask Mother. I'd love to be a fly on the wall if he tries that! Come on, stick your foot out or something — here comes the bus.'

'Please don't go to too much trouble,' Beattie Enright insisted as Jack took her coat and headed for the hall cupboard, and she followed Esther into a sitting room that looked like the aftermath of a hurricane.

'Bertie, get those toy soldiers off the settee, so that Uncle and Auntie can sit down!' Esther demanded, and Bertie obeyed with the speed of a reluctant tortoise and a facial expression that reflected the unreasonableness of the request.

'I've got a new story book from school!' Lily told Beattie before she was even seated. 'It's all about this princess who has a wicked stepmother who sends her to sleep for a hundred years until a handsome prince comes to wake her up with a kiss! You can read it to me if you like!'

'Of course, dear,' Beattie conceded, 'but why don't *you* read it to *me*, to show me how clever you are?'

'Tea?' Esther asked with a smile as she recognised the frustrated teacher in her aunt-in-law, and when Beattie nodded with a smile, Percy turned to both her and Jack.

'Let's go into the kitchen and talk while we make it.' As they walked into the kitchen, Percy asked for the diagram he'd left the previous week and began bringing it up to date. 'It looks as if we've got the Surrey side of things sewn up, and from what you were telling me yesterday, Jack, we can account for all but one of the Essex ones. The two remaining holes are the person behind the other ones in the East End and Middlesex, and of course the true identity of the person behind the whole thing.'

'Person or *persons*,' Jack reminded him. 'We've been assuming up to now that only one woman's behind them all, when in fact it might be several, acting in league with each other. Or perhaps we're dealing with separate operations with the same objective.'

'So what happened yesterday?' Percy asked.

'Frances Dickinson certainly fits the description that your Surrey witness gave you,' Jack replied, 'although whether she's also Annabelle Grant is a matter that has yet to be determined. I'm obliged to say, however, that she came across very convincingly as a senior sales assistant, and therefore probably had experience at it before she took to baby farming — if indeed she did.'

'That only goes to show how much you know about baby clothes,' Esther said condescendingly. 'Most of the items I bought were my own choice, and if I'd gone with her recommendations we'd now have a cupboard full of shoddy goods, and we'd be a whole lot poorer. And don't forget the nursing home.'

'The what?' Percy asked.

Esther continued with a proud smile. 'Your next lead. And when I say "your", I mean not me and Jack. Frances Dickinson handed us a card and a personal recommendation for an up-market nursing home in Highgate, which we suspect is a place where you can also get abortions or buy babies to your own specifications.'

'That was *my* idea!' Jack protested.

'You were the first to say it — that doesn't mean that I wasn't already thinking it,' Esther fired back. At this point the pan began bubbling furiously in a warning that if the gas weren't turned off voluntarily, the flame would be extinguished by cascading water. Esther rose from the table and poured the contents of the pan into the teapot and carried the tea things through to Beattie in the sitting room.

'Do you reckon she meant it about not going to that nursing home, at least to make an enquiry?' Percy asked. 'It could be a vital link to the baby farming, if they go in for adoptions. At the very least we might get them for performing abortions.'

'Leave Esther to me,' Jack advised him. 'She's always like a bear with a sore head at this stage of her pregnancies, but she'll pull out of it — in a couple of weeks, if it goes to form. When she comes back she's got something she wants to share with us from those additional criminal histories I ordered. I only hope it doesn't mean that we have to remember yet another name.'

Esther returned to the kitchen and Percy caught her eye.

'Jack tells me that you've made an important discovery among those latest criminal histories which he brought home on Friday.'

'It may be nothing, of course, but then again you never know, and it may be worth following up on,' Esther replied. 'One of the criminal histories related to an orphanage.'

'Which one?' Jack interrupted eagerly. 'I *knew* it was a good idea to mix all the combinations of names together and see what came out. I just didn't have time to read them all, else I would have spotted that.'

'Never mind who gets the credit,' Percy urged the pair of them, 'just tell us what you've found, Esther.'

'Well,' Esther announced with a slight preening, 'there's this woman called "Harriet Bradbury". When she was just a girl of fifteen, she and several others burned down the orphanage they had been brought up in. They were brought before the courts but let off because of their age and the tales they had to tell about what had been going on in that orphanage.'

'What had been going on?' Jack asked.

Esther shook her head. 'No idea, and even the police report states that the details were suppressed on the order of the judge.'

'I'd bet money on a deal having been done,' Percy advised them. 'They were let off, not because of their age, but in return for keeping quiet about what they'd suffered while in the orphanage. There was no Political Branch in those days, remember, and the Government was no doubt anxious to suppress any scandal regarding the ramshackle arrangements for looking after orphans, which were even worse then than they are these days. When was this exactly, Esther?'

'Almost thirty years ago, why?'

Percy's eyes lit up. 'That "Harriet Bradbury" woman and her co-offenders would now be in their middle forties, so that fits.'

'Fits what, exactly?' Jack demanded. 'What has burning down an orphanage got to do with snuffing babies?'

'No idea, at present,' Percy admitted, 'but the coincidences are too large to ignore. Ever since we started investigating this case we've been coming up with one name after another, and as we reminded ourselves five minutes ago, we've been perhaps been misleading ourselves by assuming that only one woman was involved. Supposing that the "old team", as we may call it, who burned down an orphanage for reasons unknown, has re-formed with a new mission?'

'I still don't see any connection,' Jack objected, but Esther jumped in.

'Isn't that why you're both detectives? Criminals don't come ready equipped with a full written explanation for their behaviours, nor do they advertise their reasons for committing crime in the newspapers.'

'Nicely put,' Percy said, smiling, as he made a note in his notebook. 'I'll use that one while training up new detectives, if I may. As for you, Jack, you shouldn't need reminding.'

'I didn't,' Jack sulked. 'I was just pointing out that we have more work to do, that's all.'

'Indeed you do,' Percy replied. '*Both* of you. And before you give me that look of disapproval that I know so well, Esther, how much credibility do you think Jack would have walking into a certain nursing home in Highgate and requesting further details of the services they offer?'

'You really do want us to follow up on that?' Esther pouted.

'Of course, with particular reference to whether or not they can arrange adoptions. Hang around there for as long as you can and look for signs of babies leaving with middle aged ladies who can't possibly be their mothers.'

'And if we don't meet with any success?'

'Then I might have to involve my own middle-aged lady. One more Enright to join the unofficial Scotland Yard. But I hope it doesn't come to that.'

Chapter Twelve

'Mr Greenwood will see you immediately, Inspector,' the smartly dressed lady advised Percy as she held open the door to the room she had just left. Percy thanked her with a polite smile and entered the office, behind which sat the General Manager of 'Timothy's of Oxford Street', Arnold Greenwood, a somewhat overweight individual with a round face and prominent spectacles. Percy took the seat indicated with the wave of the hand.

'So, what can I do for you, Inspector? We don't very often receive visits from Scotland Yard. In fact, I don't think I can remember one in all my years with the firm. I began as a sales assistant in Menswear, and worked my way up, you know.'

'Do all your senior staff therefore have years of service behind them before they're promoted?' Percy asked sceptically.

Greenwood nodded. 'Indeed they do. We have a policy here at Timothy's that no-one reaches a senior sales position without proving their worth in a lower position within what we like to think of as a family.'

'Except Frances Dickinson, presumably?'

'Who?'

'Frances Dickinson, Senior Sales Assistant in your "Infants and Children" department.'

'What about her?'

'You appointed her to a senior position only recently, and I have reason to believe that she's not been with you for very long.'

'What has she done, exactly?'

'Nothing, in her current position, so far as I'm aware,' Percy replied, opting to play his cards close to his chest. 'But I'd like to know more of her history before you employed her, if I may.'

'Certainly,' Greenwood replied as he reached for a button on his desk. Percy heard a buzzer sounding somewhere outside the office, and the same smartly dressed lady poked her head round the door.

'Yes, Mr Greenwood?'

'Alice, would you be so obliging as to bring in the personnel file for a…' He looked enquiringly at Percy, who completed his sentence for him.

'Frances Dickinson, "Infants and Children".'

'Yes, her, if you'd be so good,' Greenwood confirmed. 'And perhaps tea and biscuits for two?'

'Certainly, Mr Greenwood,' Alice replied obligingly as her head disappeared, and the door was closed from the other side.

'This employee of ours has been guilty of conduct outside work that might raise questions regarding her suitability as an employee of Timothy's?' Greenwood asked nervously.

Percy smiled ironically. 'Certainly the "Infants and Children" department, anyway.'

'Am I allowed to know precisely what?' Greenwood persisted. 'Here at Timothy's we're very particular in vetting our new employees. References and all the trimmings, you know?'

'Police checks?'

Greenwood looked back at him blankly. 'I wasn't aware that those were possible. So, if I'm thinking of employing a new member of staff, Scotland Yard will tell me if they've engaged in any previous criminal activity?'

'Certainly, if you ask the right people,' Percy replied with a smile. 'What did you mean by "all the trimmings", exactly?'

'Well, in addition to basic character references from respectable people in positions of authority who know the applicant personally, we like to get references from their previous employers regarding their sales record, their timekeeping and so on.'

There was what sounded like a delicate kick on the far side of the door, then a brief moment of silence before the door opened to reveal the obliging Alice struggling in with a tea tray in her hands, and a folder of some sort tucked under her armpit. Percy got up and took the tray from her, receiving her profuse thanks before she handed a thin folder to her employer, who placed it on his desk, then made a space among the remaining papers for the tea tray, which Percy put down with all the grace of a waitress in a fashionable tea house.

Greenwood poured the tea, frowned faintly when Percy requested three sugars, and pushed the plate of biscuits towards him.

'So how long has Miss Dickinson been in your employ?' Percy enquired. 'I take it that she *is* "Miss" Dickinson?'

'Let's have a look, shall we?' Greenwood suggested as he opened the file, prior to his forehead creasing in a deeper frown. 'Yes, she's unmarried,' Greenwood confirmed, 'but she's only been with us a matter of weeks. Judging by the dates, I'd hazard a guess that she was engaged by my Deputy General Manager Robert Gilbert, while I was on long-service leave. I retire next year, you know, after thirty-five years with Timothy's.'

'So, you weren't involved in hiring her from nowhere, as it were, straight into a supervisory position, without any previous service within your firm?' Percy asked with what was little short of a smirk.

Greenwood looked embarrassed as he perused the file in more detail. 'Not personally, no. But her predecessor had died suddenly and tragically, when she was knocked down by a bus while leaving work one afternoon. Very distressing for the staff who witnessed it, obviously.'

'And that left you in urgent need of a replacement?' Percy prompted him.

Greenwood nodded. 'Precisely. And to judge by this reference, we were extremely fortunate that Miss Dickinson applied for a position when she did. It's one of the best I've ever read, and it comes from the Sales Director of "Burwoods Drapery" in Knightsbridge, one of our rivals in haberdashery. He even took the trouble to write it by hand.'

'Might I see it, please?' Percy requested.

Greenwood handed it across the desk, then looked puzzled when Percy extracted a second document from his jacket pocket and compared the two.

'Were you aware that the Sales Director of that rival firm you mentioned is also in holy orders?' Percy said with a wide smirk.

'How do you mean?'

'Well, while I'm not an official handwriting expert,' Percy replied, 'I've got quite handy at it over the years, and to my experienced eye the person who wrote this glowing reference for your Miss Dickinson when she applied for employment here is the same individual who was calling himself the Vicar of Oxshott when Miss Dickinson, using another name altogether, was applying for the tenancy of a house in Cobham, in Surrey, which she vacated in circumstances that are currently the subject of police enquiries.'

'You mean she supplied us with a forged reference?' Greenwood demanded, his face a picture of outrage. 'I'll have her dismissed immediately!'

'I'd rather you didn't,' Percy requested, 'since while she's working here at least I know where to find her when I want her. In the meantime, console yourself with the prospect that the person who supplied this reference — which incidentally I'd like to retain, if I may — also conducts Sunday services in Oxshott as a bogus church minister. Tell the charming Alice that I'll see myself out.'

The day had been pretty good so far, but Percy wasn't necessarily looking forward to the next part of it. Neither was Chief Superintendent Bray, to judge by the stern expression on his face that made Percy wonder whether he knew something that Percy didn't.

'Well, it's been a month, near enough, so, where are we? They're short of a senior man in Fraud at the moment, so it had better be convincing.'

'It's actually even more "Political Branch" than I first imagined,' Percy urged upon him. 'There's a network of women preying on the desperation of some girls to get rid of unwanted babies, and other childless women to acquire them.'

'A trade in infants, you mean?' Bray said. 'If the demand meets the supply, and we go wading in there disrupting the terms of trade, there'll almost certainly be a political uproar, so tread carefully.

'Indeed I will, sir, but you should also be advised that the supply outstrips demand most of the time, hence the depressing prevalence of infant corpses, not only on our patch, but in Middlesex, Surrey and Essex. Probably elsewhere as well.'

'I have it on good authority from a very aggrieved officer of equivalent rank in Essex that you've got your nephew involved as well. That knowledge has the capacity to tweak my ulcer, so tell me it isn't true, if you dare.'

'Detective Sergeant Enright is the very officer assigned to investigate the discovery of infant corpses in Essex, sir, and like the resourceful officers that we both are we've combined our efforts, and it's already bearing fruit.'

'Convince me.'

'Well, first of all, Sergeant Enright has already discovered who was dumping the bodies on his patch, and from her he's got the name — or rather, the "names" — of the woman who supplied the babies for disposal.'

'And you've got her buckled?'

'Not yet, sir, because we haven't tracked her down. But we believe that she's part of a network of women in the same criminal enterprise, one of whom was until recently blocking the drains of a house in Cobham with dead babies but is now working as a sales assistant in a West End department store — in the "Infants and Children's Department", unfortunately.'

'Dear God,' Bray moaned, 'if the newspapers get hold of that we'll be laughed out of Whitehall. Pull her in immediately!'

'If I might sound a note of caution on that point, sir…'

'That was an order, Detective Inspector, not a suggestion! Are we agreed on that?'

'Yes sir, but it might get in the way of some other delicate enquiries.'

'Such as?'

'Well, the lady in question has given us a lead to a nursing home in Highgate which we believe may be the new centre of operations for the baby farming business. They had to move from the house they were using in Surrey at short notice, but while they were still in business there they were using totties from the city to get rid of the bodies. I believe that the dead bodies left in the drains were the consequence of a panicked departure before they could call the girls in to do a final disposal. But the fact that the girls were being drawn from their usual haunts in the East End suggests that the Surrey house was the main one, and that the East End was only a convenient dumping ground. Now that they've had to shut up shop in Surrey, I believe that they've reopened in Highgate.'

'But this woman you mentioned, who gave you the lead to this Highgate house, has served her purpose, has she not?'

'In that sense, yes, sir.'

'Then pull her in — understood?'

'Yes sir, except that if we do, might it not alert those in Highgate that we've rumbled them? If so, they'll just move on, presumably with more blocked drains on the way out.'

'That's your problem.'

'Yes, sir.'

'And this house in Highgate, presumably you're going to raid it?'

'Not yet, sir.'

'And why not, if you have good evidence that it's being used for this ghastly trade, and before we get more blocked drains that will be fairly and squarely our responsibility this time?'

'Well, sir,' Percy explained as patiently as he could, 'all we have is a referral to it, and no actual proof that it's being used for anything unlawful. I thought we might do a little undercover investigation to test our suspicions before we go blundering in with whistles, rattles and handcuffs.'

'And how do you propose to do that, exactly? You can hardly expect even the prettiest of our men to pose as a woman seeking to adopt a baby, or indeed to get rid of one.'

'I have that point covered, sir.'

'I'd be intrigued to learn how.'

'Well, sir, at the risk of provoking your ulcer, I've got Jack Enright lined up to assist in that.'

'From memory, your nephew's over six feet tall. Hardly credible as a pregnant woman, is he?'

'No, sir, but his wife's pregnant again.'

'He's clearly getting too much time off. And isn't she the woman you involved in several previous enquiries that ended badly?'

'Depends how you define "badly", sir. She helped us identify "The Ripper", she was instrumental in landing us that man who murdered his sister and dumped her body in a railway tunnel, and more recently she helped to expose the man behind the frauds over the Bethnal Green slum demolitions.'

'When I say "badly", Enright, I'm referring to the unfortunate fact that whenever you get involved in an undercover operation with the Enrights, we somehow finish up without a suspect to put on trial. May I remind you of the unfortunate circumstances in which one of our prime suspects finished up under a coal train?'

'You don't need to remind me, sir, since I'm unlikely to ever forget the sight.'

'And that thug in Bethnal Green — you arranged for the mob to rip him apart before we even got him on remand, did you not?'

'An unfortunate lapse of prisoner security, sir.'

'Unfortunate for him, certainly. And now you're proposing to send Enright and his wife into this baby farm that you're investigating? How do I know that it won't mysteriously go up in flames or something?'

'You have my guarantee on that, sir. Jack Enright and his wife will simply have a look around, on the pretence of booking her in for her confinement, which incidentally isn't until September. If we get a whiff that there are babies for sale by adoption, then I intend to go in myself for the next stage.'

'Alone?'

'No sir — with my own wife, although I'd appreciate it if you'd keep that information to yourself, since I haven't asked her yet.'

'You have to "ask", rather than "inform"?'

'If you'd met my wife, you'd know why, sir, but that's a little way down the tracks yet. In the meantime, I'd be grateful if you'd let me allow this Dickinson woman — she's the one from the Cobham house, remember, the one who gave us the lead to the Highgate house? — to remain where she is. If she suspects that we're on to her, she'll alert the Highgate people, and then I strongly suspect that more blocked drains will be the order of the day.'

Bray sat for a moment, deep in thought, then shook his head. 'Sorry, Percy, but I can't take the risk that the newspapers will get wind of the fact that we allowed a woman suspected of systematically murdering babies to continue selling infant clothing in the West End. Pull her in without delay.'

'And the Highgate house?'

'Do whatever you need to do. But don't bugger it up and leave us with egg on our faces.'

'Just promise me that I won't actually have to give birth here,' Esther pleaded weakly as she and Jack gazed up at the impressive three storey facade of the largest house in the leafiest street in Highgate. It was another Saturday morning — a week after their trip into the West End to 'Timothy's' — and

Esther was far from convinced that this was a good idea.

'Of course not,' Jack assured her as he took her hand and pulled her gently through the ornate gateway and up the path lined with rose bushes towards the glass front door, above which was what looked like a temporary sign — or at least, one that had only recently been commissioned in a hurry — that read 'Highgate Manor'.

Once through the door there was only one obvious place to go, and that was up to what looked like a reception desk on the far side of an elegantly furnished entrance lounge, with coffee tables on which brochures were laid out for consumption by whoever sat in one of the plush chairs. Jack was just wondering if perhaps they had got the wrong place, or if this institution was on the level after all, when the young woman behind the reception desk rose from her seat and beamed encouragingly at them.

'Good morning, I'm Nurse Pemberton. How may I be of assistance?'

'I'm expecting my first in September,' Esther croaked with a nervousness that might have been genuine in the circumstances, 'and this place was recommended by a lady who served us with baby clothes in a West End department store last week.'

'"This place", as you call it,' the woman replied somewhat haughtily, 'is indeed a nursing home that specialises in a full birthing experience. You might wish to peruse our scale of fees,' she added as she pushed a single printed sheet of paper across the counter towards them, with a facial expression that implied that the fees might be beyond their capacity to pay. Both Jack and Esther managed to keep a straight face as they perused the totally outrageous price list, Esther calculating in her head that she could feed the entire family for three months on the money that was required — in advance, as the brochure was careful to specify in italics at its foot — for a three day stay, with midwifery fees additional.

'So, when were you think of being admitted?' the snooty one enquired.

Jack's humour got the better of him. 'We thought perhaps we might choose a date that coincided with the birth,' he chirped, to a frozen face behind the desk.

'My question was rather when the baby's due,' was the reply he deserved, and Esther decided that it was time she did the talking.

'My private doctor in Bedford Square believes that it will be in late August or early September, but he recommended that I book into a clinic without delay, to ensure that I'm properly cared for when the time comes. It's our first, you see, and we've waited quite a while. We were recommended to you by the Senior Sales Assistant at "Timothy's of Oxford Street". A Miss Dickinson, whose cousin owns this establishment.'

'The proprietor is also our Senior Matron,' the woman replied, seemingly unfazed. 'I have no knowledge of any relations she may have in the garment trade. However, let's record a few details, shall we, if our scale of fees is commensurate with your budget.'

'We hadn't thought to budget for something as important as our first child,' Esther replied frostily, 'but I saw nothing on your price list that caused me any concern.'

'"Scale of fees", not "price list",' the woman replied with a rigid smile. 'If you'd like to take these application forms over to the seating area behind you there, and supply the required details, I'll take you through to meet Matron.'

'Stuck up cow!' Esther muttered as they took a seat and she reached for one of the pens that sat in ornate ink stands on the table in front of her.

'This is certainly a lot posher that I'd expected,' Jack whispered. 'I think it may be a genuine nursing home; it's certainly hard to imagine any illicit trade in unwanted babies born to "quite the wrong sort of girl".'

'Keep your voice down,' Esther hissed urgently. 'That pompous baggage on the front desk already thinks you're not quite worthy of being the father of my child. Now, where do we live?'

'Use the old address in Clerkenwell,' Jack suggested.

Esther shook her head. 'Not grand enough. But I can remember the address of that dreadful gallery in Hatton Garden where I worked for that creepy art dealer, so that'll do. Now, what do you work as? I can hardly put down that you're a policeman, can I?'

'Detective Sergeant,' Jack corrected her, 'but when we bought those baby clothes I pretended that I was an architect, so put that down.'

'How much do you earn a week?'

Jack grinned. 'In my pretended profession, my dear, one speaks in terms of "annual salary", not "so many pounds a week". Call it eleven hundred a year.'

'You're kidding, surely?' Esther protested. 'You don't look as if you're worth that much.'

'Thank you,' Jack replied sarcastically, just as his attention was drawn to a middle-aged couple who had entered the reception area by way of the front door and sidled, with guilty facial expressions, up to the reception desk, where the man muttered something almost under his breath and the reception nurse beamed back at him.

'Certainly, Mr Grainger. I'll tell Matron Merchant that you're here.'

Jack dug Esther in the ribs and indicated with a head gesture for her to pay attention to what was happening at the front desk. The receptionist slid out from behind her counter and walked to a door to her left that had no notice on it to indicate who might be inside. She tapped discreetly on the door, then poked her head round it following what was presumably an invitation to enter.

'Matron will see you immediately,' she called to the couple, who stepped eagerly towards her. As the door was pushed further open it revealed a lady in her early forties rising from behind her desk to welcome her visitors. In a flash Jack took in her lack of height and her severely cut black hair. He was willing to bet that she also had piercing black eyes, but she was too far away to tell, and the door closed quickly behind the new arrivals.

'Yes!' Jack hissed.

'Yes what?' Esther said in a whispered conspiratorial tone.

Jack leaned forward and kissed her on the cheek. 'The couple who went in there are *far* too old for her to be requiring "birthing facilities". Almost certainly they're here for an adoption. And the woman behind the desk in there — the Matron who's also the proprietor, according to "Snooty Knickers" — fits the description of both Martha Bradbury *and* Harriet Merchant. Our day wasn't completely wasted, it seems. Now it's up to Uncle Percy.'

The man in question was, at approximately the same time, swearing his way down Oxford Street in the company of a uniformed constable who was greatly amused and trying not to show it. Not only did he have nothing further to do until they got back to the Yard and he was allocated further patrol duties, but he was thoroughly enjoying the discomfort of the overbearing bugger who'd been treating him like a personal valet all morning.

Percy had waited as long as he'd dared before returning to Timothy's on the Saturday morning, clutching an arrest warrant, with a uniformed bobby to do the 'hands on' part of the operation. He'd walked smartly up to the front counter of the "Infants and Children" department, waved his police badge high in the air and announced to the undivided attention of everyone in there that he wished to speak to Miss Dickinson.

There was an embarrassed silence until a middle-aged sales assistant advised him, in a hushed voice, that Miss Dickinson was no longer in the employ of 'Timothy's of Oxford Street'.

'You mean she was sacked?' Percy thundered.

'Of course not. She resigned. Today was meant to be her last day with us, but she didn't show up for work this morning.'

Chapter Thirteen

'Mary Draycott was asking if cheese scones would be appropriate for your cake stall,' Constance Enright told Esther as they sipped their tea after enjoying another splendid Sunday dinner prepared by a cook and served by a housemaid who were now exchanging gossip over their own pot of tea in the kitchen.

Esther thought for a moment before offering her opinion. 'They're not really "cakes" of the traditional sort, but the more the merrier, I suppose.'

'If they don't sell well,' Percy said, grinning, 'I'll underwrite them for you and buy the lot.'

'Will you and Aunt Beattie be coming to the Summer Fair?' Esther asked hopefully.

Beattie shook her head. 'Probably not, and you're the main reason.' When Esther looked hurt, Beattie smiled and explained her reasoning. 'If Percy were to be let loose anywhere near a cake stall, I'd need a wheelbarrow to get him back to the station.'

'Unkind,' Percy muttered, 'but talking of trains, we'll need to be leaving soon.'

'So will we,' Jack added. 'I'll just go and prise Lily and Bertie off the swing.'

Ten minutes later the family party set off up Church Lane and past the church yard in which the 'Summer Fayre' was now being advertised. As usual, Lily and Bertie ran ahead of the adults, receiving regular admonitions from Esther not to go out of sight, while she and Jack walked more slowly alongside Percy and Beattie with baby Miriam in the perambulator.

'I always feel so guilty when we do this,' Beattie complained. 'You know, turning right to go to your house, rather than left for the station? If Constance ever finds out, I wouldn't know where to put my face.'

'It's all in a good cause,' Percy reminded her. 'Now that Jack's based in Chelmsford we only get these brief opportunities to get together and discuss a case, and if I have to justify myself to Constance, it'll be on the ground that she doesn't allow us to talk about work during her Sunday dinners.'

'You can see her point, though,' Jack argued. 'It's not as if the things we're obliged to talk about are all that pleasant or uplifting in content, and this latest one is really very distressing — all those dead babies.'

'I don't know much about it, obviously,' Beattie reminded them as Bertie ran back and grabbed her hand in an effort to drag her ahead into Bunting Lane, 'but it certainly sounds horrible, to judge by the little bit I've heard. But if you boys need time together to discuss a case, why can't you do it during working hours?'

'Too many distractions,' Percy replied.

Jack nodded his agreement. 'Particularly in my case,' he added, 'since everything to do with detective work lands on my desk first. It's like Paddington Station in my office some days, although I can usually pass most of it down to my constables. But this latest one's too big and complex for them, and given the links with the Met's patch, I'm the obvious one to work alongside Uncle Percy.'

There was a three-foot drainage ditch of sorts that ran all the way down the left-hand side of Bunting Lane, which was crossed by means of a wooden plank that had grown a little rickety over the years and required the pram to be lifted in order to cross it. Percy and Jack took an end each, while Esther walked quickly ahead of them down the drive and unlocked the scullery door. As she lit the gas for a pot of tea and lifted the covers off the plate of sandwiches that she'd prepared earlier that day, Beattie headed into the garden to supervise Bertie on one of the rare occasions that he was allowed the use of the swing, and Lily opted to pick flowers for one of the several vases that adorned their house.

While the pan was boiling, and with stern instructions to Jack and Percy to leave some sandwiches for Beattie, Esther opened the discussions.

'As Jack couldn't resist telling you over sherry, while his mother was giving the cook her last minutes instructions, we're pretty certain that the woman in charge of the Highgate nursing home is the same woman who was organising the disposal of dead babies here in Essex.'

'Yes,' Jack added, 'and I discovered, while investigating another matter entirely, that a local totty — name of Clara Bristow — was the person who'd dumped all the babies on my patch with the exception of the one that probably floated downriver from yours. She was, to cut a long story short, blackmailed into it by a local woman calling herself "Martha Bradley". Then, thanks to Esther that same woman was described to me as "Harriet Merchant", the name she was using in previous years when she apparently had a legitimate interest in finding good homes for infants before they became orphans on the street. The description in both cases is a very distinctive one — small in height, with close cropped dark hair, almost like a nun, and with dark penetrating eyes. When we turned up at the place at Highgate, and while we were filling in forms, this middle-aged couple walked in, looking pretty furtive, to my mind anyway, and were shown into the office of the so-called "Matron" of the place, who fitted that description perfectly, from the little I saw of her.'

'A middle-aged couple, you say?' Percy said thoughtfully.

'Precisely,' Jack answered. 'The perfect customers for an adoption.'

'In a way I was hoping that you wouldn't say that,' Percy grimaced. 'I now have to persuade your Aunt Beattie to come with me.'

'It'll make a change for some other female member of the Enright family to get their hands dirty,' Esther observed. 'You're forever getting me involved and a couple of times you've dragged Lucy into it, so it must be Beattie's turn.'

'Would you care to be the person to tell her?' Percy asked gloomily.

Esther shook her head with a smile.

'So where have you got to, Uncle?' Jack said eagerly.

Percy seemed to perk up as he supplied the latest from his side of the investigation. 'We were obviously right about that Frances Dickinson who referred you to the nursing home, who was almost certainly, of course, Annabelle Grant in Surrey. It seems that she only joined the staff of "Timothy's" recently, using a forged reference. That would tie in with the date of her abrupt departure from the Surrey adoption agency, leaving dead babies in the drains. In her new role she was of course ideally placed to point pregnant women in the direction of Highgate.'

'So you know where to find her when we throw the net over the Highgate place that has presumably replaced the Surrey operation?' Jack enquired.

Percy frowned. 'That's the bad news. Somebody must have tipped Frances Dickinson off regarding my enquiries with the General Manager of Timothy's. Whoever it was, it did the trick, because she resigned and didn't even show up for work on her final day, when I was all set to buckle her.'

'Something that's been puzzling me,' Esther intervened as she laid out the tea things on the table, 'is how this woman calling herself Annabelle Grant at the time knew that it was time to fly the coop from the house in Surrey. Someone must have tipped her off about her place being under scrutiny, surely?'

'Well, we have to assume that it wasn't us, anyway,' Percy replied. 'And I'm embarrassed to admit that the point never occurred to me. It must have been one of the neighbours, and I'm obviously due a return visit to Cobham.'

Just then the scullery door opened noisily, and Bertie raced in through the kitchen. When he became aware of the sandwiches on the table, he said, 'Are there any eggy ones?' before plunging his grubby hands into the pile.

'Bertie!' Esther yelled, 'go and wash your hands before you handle any food! Then, and only then, we'll find you an eggy one.'

As Bertie raced towards the bathroom at the only speed he seemed to be capable of, Beattie and Lily came into the kitchen at a more sedate pace.

'Do you have any spare vases, dear?' Beattie asked Esther. 'Lily's picked some lovely late daffodils and it would be a shame not to have them displayed in the house before they finally wilt.'

'I'll see to that while you help yourself to tea and sandwiches, before the gannets finish them off,' Esther said, smiling, before congratulating Lily on her choice of blooms and escorting her towards the cupboard in the hall where assorted containers were kept. Once they had disappeared through the kitchen door, Jack looked mischievously across at his Aunt Beattie, who was pouring herself a cup of tea.

'I believe that Uncle Percy has a favour to ask of you,' he said, as Percy glared back at him.

'You mean not divorcing him?' Beattie replied acidly.

'Not quite, although it might come to that,' Jack chuckled.

'You'd better leave this to me,' Percy warned.

'Leave *what* to you, dear?' Beattie asked suspiciously.

Percy swallowed hard before beginning one of the hardest tasks of his entire career. 'Do you remember, before Constance very kindly allowed Jack to come and live with us, how we seriously considered adoption?'

'Of course I do,' Beattie replied stonily, 'and there are days — which today seems to be turning into — when I wish we'd continued down that path, rather than recruit someone who'd follow you into the police force and get you into even more trouble. So, what are you getting at?'

'And you know how occasionally Esther has proved invaluable in solving a case, and on two occasions I've recruited Lucy as well?'

'More fool them — what's your point, Percy? Or is this some sort of guessing game?'

'It's very hard to explain in simple terms...' Percy began, before Esther reappeared immediately behind him clutching a vase, accompanied by Lily holding a bunch of daffodils, and took the opportunity to get her own back for past impositions.

'He means that it's your turn, Aunt Beattie. Uncle Percy wants to use you like he's used me in the past — to catch criminals.'

'Out of the question!' Beattie exclaimed. 'I haven't forgotten the terrible risks that you've exposed poor Esther to in the past — are you trying to get rid of me or something?'

'Definitely not,' Percy insisted with a sideways glare at Esther. 'But you'd be perfect for something I have to do. Something I can't do on my own.'

'You want me to pose as a lady of the streets or something equally undignified?' Beattie demanded, hands on hips.

Esther decided that it was time she lent a hand. 'Uncle Percy's never even used *me* for that, Aunt Beattie. I think he has in mind that you pose as a woman seeking to adopt a child.'

'At *my* age?' Beattie countered.

Percy nodded. 'Precisely because of your age. There's a so-called nursing home in Highgate that we believe may be a cover for unofficial adoptions, and I need to go in there and investigate whether or not that's the case. If I went in by myself — a man in his fifties, seemingly single — they'd probably write me off as a filthy old pervert seeking a young child for all the wrong reasons. But with you by my side, posing as a couple who've clearly passed the childbearing age and desperate to adopt, we might get somewhere.'

'I'll have to think about it very carefully,' Beattie replied, 'but right now I have to put Bertie to bed, and check that the beautiful Miriam's sleeping soundly, so if you'd excuse me...' She passed sedately through into the hall, heading for the nursery in which Miriam was hopefully in dreamworld, and Jack grinned as he closed the kitchen door behind her and looked at Percy.

'That could have gone a lot worse. When do you intend to tell her that your real mission is to catch a woman who murders babies and gets totties to dispose of their corpses?'

'I obviously have not the slightest intention of telling her that,' Percy replied sternly, 'and if *you* do, rest assured that I'll spare no effort in having you reduced to Constable rank and allocated to supervisory duties in the local cattle market.'

Chapter Fourteen

Two days later, Percy walked up the front path of Alfred Boothroyd's house and surgery and heard the sound of childish laughter from somewhere to the rear of the house. Since one branch of the path wound its way down the side of the building, Percy followed it and found himself on a large, well-tended, lawn, on which a girl of about five years of age was bowling a hoop around in circles and giggling with glee. Alfred and Ethel Boothroyd sat in deckchairs at the top of the lawn, a table full of glassware between them, smiling happily at the young girl's antics.

As Percy walked towards them, Ethel Boothroyd rose with a worried expression, said something to her husband, and nodded towards Percy.

'Absolutely nothing to concern yourselves about,' Percy assured them as he walked across, then smiled down the lawn at the girl. 'Is that Sarah?'

Alfred nodded. 'She should be at school, I know, but she had a slight fever yesterday and Dr Meredith advised that she be kept at home for a day or two. Being Sarah, of course, she's overdoing it as usual, but what can we do for you, since I assume that you're not here to watch our daughter chasing a hoop around the garden?'

'No indeed,' Percy replied, smiling. 'It's just that I'm a little puzzled as to how Annabelle Grant, as you knew her, came to realise that the time had come to close down her adoption agency and move on.'

Alfred Boothroyd's face fell and Ethel broke the silence to enquire if Percy would like a glass of home-made lemonade.

He accepted with gratitude and took the remaining seat as Ethel poured him a glass and her husband began his embarrassed admission.

'It was highly irregular of me, I freely admit, and if you could refrain from passing on what I'm about to tell you to my colleagues in the local community group, I'd consider it a great favour.'

'You warned her, didn't you?' Percy said in what he hoped was an encouraging tone of voice.

Alfred nodded. 'Yes, I did, but not officially. When the letters of complaint began to come in from that frightful nosey parker Emily Talbot, the other members of my committee voted that she should be sent a formal letter of warning regarding the recent goings on at her establishment. I persuaded our Secretary to leave the task to me, without disclosing my reasons, and then I called round to Miss Grant's house in person late one evening and explained the position. She seemed genuinely concerned to learn that her "activities", shall we call them, had attracted adverse criticism, and even went so far as to assure me that the young ladies who were coming and going were potential adoption clients of hers. I had no reason to doubt that they were and, as you'd appreciate, I considered that after the wonderful service she'd performed for us in finding us Sarah, it was the least that I owed her to give her a gentle informal warning. Believe me, no-one was more horrified than me to learn what had really been going on in there, and I'm very conscious of the fact that I was derelict in my duty towards the residents' group, but I honestly believed that I was acting in everyone's best interests — including that old mischief-maker Emily Talbot.'

Percy smiled reassuringly. 'No-one could criticise your actions, Mr Boothroyd, and I thank you for your frankness.

Without your explanation I would have been harbouring suspicions that someone on the local police force had acted corruptly. I take it that you never contacted the police regarding the goings on at the adoption agency?'

'Of course not — why would I?'

'Indeed, and as it turned out, they got involved soon enough.'

'Is there any more news in that direction?' Ethel enquired.

Percy smiled again. 'Only to confirm that you were almost certainly correct in your identification of the woman calling herself "Frances Dickinson" as the same woman who was calling herself "Annabelle Grant" when she was your neighbour.'

'And our very good friend and saviour,' Alfred reminded him. 'I hope you'll go easy on her now that I assume she's been arrested.'

'I'm afraid she hasn't, Mr Boothroyd,' Percy advised him as the smile disappeared from his face. 'She was just one cog in a much larger wheel, but we have plans afoot to stop that particular wheel from turning in the very near future.'

'I still can't quite believe that you talked me into this, Percy,' Beattie grumbled as she looked up at the impressive building in Highgate that to her mind belonged in the occupation of some leading lawyer or successful politician, and not a sordid trader in other people's unwanted offspring. Then she reminded herself of how close she and Percy had come to resorting to a place like this, took a deep breath, and followed Percy up the driveway.

'Let me do all the talking,' Percy muttered as they rang the front door bell.

'Why wouldn't I?' Beattie replied with a hiss, 'since you normally do anyway. I just hope that it's not too unpleasant in there.'

The door was opened by a smiling woman in her mid-thirties, dressed in a lilac-coloured smock. 'May I help you?' she enquired through her smile without seemingly moving her lips.

'We hope so,' Percy replied. 'Might it be possible for us to speak with your Matron Merchant?'

'In connection with *what*, exactly? May I assume that you're not here to enquire about birthing facilities — or is it for your daughter, perhaps?'

'It's a personal and confidential matter, and one of some delicacy,' Percy muttered, trying to look shamefaced.

'One moment,' the woman requested as she closed the door in their faces.

Beattie made a disgusted noise in her throat. 'This is so demeaning, Percy. I feel as if I'm here for an abortion or something.'

'Too late for that,' Percy chuckled, 'but I'll guarantee that this front door will swing wide open for us in no time at all.'

When he was proved right after less than a minute, the lady with the painted-on smile ushered them into an office to the right of the front counter, where they were greeted effusively by 'Matron Merchant', who was exactly as described by Jack.

'I was advised by Nurse Carrington that you wished to speak with me,' Matron oozed as she gestured them into the chairs in front of her office desk. 'What would that be in connection with, exactly?'

Percy allowed himself a nervous cough and a downward drop of the eyes before proceeding. 'You operate a birth clinic here, do you not?'

'Yes, clearly. If I might delicately ask on whose behalf you are making these enquiries? And is it perhaps a matter that must be treated with discretion?'

'Not in our case, no,' Percy persevered in a hushed voice. 'But might we enquire whether or not, from time to time, there are young ladies who give birth here for whom the burden of a child might prove too daunting a prospect, or perhaps even a social inconvenience?'

'Let's not walk around each other any longer, Mr…?'

'Jackson. Percy Jackson. And this is my wife Beatrice.'

Beattie duly obliged with downcast eyes, not quite believing that she was actually participating in this breath-taking display of embarrassment and modesty by the arrogant bombast she'd been married to for over thirty years.

'You're seeking to adopt, are you not?' Matron demanded bluntly.

Percy executed the humblest nod Beattie had ever witnessed.

'Well,' Matron continued encouragingly, 'it is true that from time to time — only occasionally, you understand, but from time to time — we are asked by one of our clients to make enquiries into the possibility that someone entirely suitable might be willing to relieve them of the consequence of an indiscretion that could prove "socially inconvenient", to adopt your expression.'

'That was what we were hoping,' Percy replied humbly. 'Could you place us on your list of potential recipients?'

'I *could*,' Matron replied, 'but you must appreciate that this is not exactly a "bring and buy sale" that we're talking about. We take great pride, here at Highgate House, in ensuring that the child is matched with a couple who are in all ways suited to it. In terms of education, social status, financial security, and so on. And since most of the young ladies who are obliged, for the best of reasons, to part with the consequences of childbirth, are from the upper echelons of society, we have to be very selective in the choice of adoptive parents.'

'I quite understand,' Percy replied. 'I am now retired from my former profession of dentistry, and both Beatrice and I are in our mid-fifties. God has not chosen to bless us with offspring, and as the result our house in Hampstead has always seemed to lack something. It was our dearest wish to have a daughter of our own, but given that this has not proved possible, it seemed to us that our best step forward might be to adopt some child whose life under the less than tender care of a reluctant mother might be improved by its translation into a more loving environment in which she would lack for nothing. I say "she" because our preference would be for a girl.'

'You appreciate that there are certain administrative processes to be observed, for which a fee would be required?'

Percy nodded. 'Naturally, we would be more than content to make a contribution to the work of your worthy establishment...'

'Two hundred pounds,' Matron interrupted bluntly.

Percy managed to keep the astonishment from his face at both the size of the fee and the bare-faced confidence with which it had been demanded. He'd obviously done a good job in playing the part of the desperate and wealthy seeker after an adoptive child and was now reaping the consequences. If he'd seemed more reluctant, the amount demanded would no doubt have been much lower, but he was committed now and ploughed on. 'Would you require that in cash? And when, precisely?'

'As for the "when", that will depend upon a suitable child becoming available. We'll be in touch in due course, should that occur, and it might then be easier for payment to be made in readily negotiable currency when you call to collect the child, assuming that this turns out to be the case. You would, I think, concede that in the circumstances payment by cheque or some other negotiable bill would not be entirely appropriate.'

'Indeed not,' Percy agreed, as he reached out to squeeze Beattie's hand in a gesture designed to imply joyful gratitude.

'We normally require a ten per cent deposit,' Percy was informed.

He frowned. 'I was led to believe, from our previous conversation,' he replied, 'that the availability of an unwanted child is a rare occurrence in this establishment. How, therefore, can the requirement for a deposit be regarded as "normal"? Do you engage in a wholesale trade here?'

'No, of course not,' Matron replied with a red face. 'An unfortunate choice of words, and in the circumstances, it will be appropriate for payment to be made in full when and if a suitable child should become available. But I *will* require a home or confidential business address, should that happy day eventuate.'

'Naturally,' Percy conceded with a renewed smile, as he took the pen and paper that was pushed across the table towards him and wrote something down. They were shown out with a good deal more deference than they had been shown in with, and as they walked hand in hand down the front path Percy was chuckling to himself. Eventually he turned to look at Beattie and advised her, 'You can let go of my hand now.'

'I don't want to,' she replied, smiling.

'But we no longer have to keep up the pretence,' he reminded her.

'Who's pretending?' she said as she leaned forward and kissed him. 'I saw another side to you in there, Percy Enright, and one which re-opened the space in my heart that you own, but don't regularly visit.'

It fell quiet as they walked down to the corner, where the police coach was waiting, suitably concealed behind a stand of trees, to take them home. Then something occurred to Beattie. 'Talking of home, what address did you give that awful woman?'

Percy laughed. 'I enjoyed that most of all. Her letter — should she ever send one — will be delivered to Hampstead Police Station.'

There was more good news for Percy when he arrived for work the following morning. According to the note on his desk, there had been a telephone call from the police station in Commercial Street, Shoreditch, requesting that Percy contact an Inspector Dalgleish.

He walked down to the Control Room in order to access one of the few telephones that existed inside the Yard and after dialling the number supplied on the large sheet that covered the side wall and asking to speak with the man in question, he was advised that a street prostitute called Mabel Barker had some valuable information to exchange in return for not being processed on a charge of Attempted Murder — information that had to do with the regular distribution of infant bodies around the East End.

Chapter Fifteen

'This may be the very breakthrough we've been looking for,' a very appreciative Percy Enright smiled at Inspector Hamish Dalgleish across his desk on the upper floor of Commercial Street Police Station, the clatter of the morning traffic below them partly deadened by the closed window that was in dire need of a good wash.

'Don't build yeir hopes up,' Dalgleish replied in the soft Edinburgh burr that was still identifiable enough to have earned him the nickname 'Jock', but not to his face. 'If the lass an' her man can't talk their way oot o' this, the pair o' them may swing tergether.'

'So how did they come to be offering all this information?' Percy enquired.

Dalgleish pushed the report across the desk towards him. 'Read it fae yersel' — it's pretty full.'

Percy allowed his eyes to run down the hastily handwritten report from the constable who'd arrested Mabel Barker and Thomas Freestone two evenings previously on serious, if depressingly familiar, charges. Mabel was a run of the mill prostitute, but she operated in league with her de facto partner Freestone in a common dodge. Mabel would lure a prosperous looking 'mark' into a dark alleyway — the same one every time, between the back of the bootmaker's shop and the front of the ironmongers. Once they got down to 'the business', Freestone would creep up behind them and present a knife to the throat of the unsuspecting 'client' and rob him of all that he was carrying.

The vast majority of their victims simply accepted that they had been well and truly duped and were glad to have emerged from the robbery with their lives; there was also the additional embarrassment of the circumstances in which it had occurred. For these reasons, Mabel and Tommy had been getting away with it for years.

Then came the night when they picked on entirely the wrong mark, a soldier from a Guards regiment who was indignant enough to report what had happened to him and determined enough to take plain-clothed officers back to the pub in which he'd first picked up Mabel and identify the pair of them. A simple undercover operation involving one of those officers, posing as a 'mark' for Mabel and followed covertly into the same alleyway by several colleagues, had netted the pair of them.

A vindictive Inspector Dalgleish had opted to charge the pair of them with Attempted Murder, which still carried the death penalty. The motive was to deter anyone else from engaging in the same activity, which was becoming all too prevalent on his patch, particularly in the railway carriages that were left nightly in the sidings of Shoreditch Station to be hitched to the first train of the following day. For several years these carriages had become the location of choice for street prostitutes seeking to offer their clients a greater degree of comfort than a back alley could provide, and once they were effectively trapped inside a carriage that had only one set of doors, it was too easy for the girl's partner in crime to commit the robbery.

Horrified at the prospect of ending their days on the end of a rope, probably at the same time, side by side, Freestone and Mabel had decided to barter for their lives in return for a reduced charge of simple robbery. It was at this point that Mabel opted to play her master card and reveal the occasions when she had earned an extra shilling by creeping into secluded spots and leaving infant corpses to be discovered by horrified local residents.

Down in the cells, Percy asked himself yet again how anyone could be so desperate for a sexual encounter that they would go up a back alley with someone as ugly, and foul smelling, as Mabel Barker. Then again, he reasoned, those men who chose such options were invariably drunk at the time, and the girl of their choice had probably doused herself with cheap perfume. He also took into account that Mabel had now been confined in a cell for almost two days, and the perfume, although still faintly detectable, was — like Mabel herself — well past its best.

'You the copper what needs to 'ear sumfin' important?' Mabel asked with all the aggression that girls like her possessed when they weren't sidling up to a mark.

'I'm certainly here to listen to what you might have to tell me,' Percy replied with a faint smile as he made a big show of extracting the notebook and pencil from his top pocket.

'Wot's it werf?'

'That depends upon what you have to tell me, doesn't it?' Percy replied with a caution born of years of negotiating with criminals.

'If it's werf sumfin, Tommy an' me won't 'ang, that right?'

'Try me.'

'Well, me an' a few o' the gals round 'ere earns a few extra bob from time ter time by gettin' rid o' dead babies fer this obligin' lady. Them's dead when we gets 'em, understood? We only dumps 'em somewhere outa the way, like, an' gals like us, well we knows where all the dark places is, don't we?'

'Tell me where you dumped the last one,' Percy insisted with his best cynical facial expression.

'In a railway carriage, up the station,' Mabel replied without hesitation, 'but that were a couple o' weeks back now. I reckon the lady's due back 'ere soon, 'cos it 'appens every few weeks.'

'Which pub?' Percy demanded, pencil poised.

'The Unicorn, corner o' the 'Igh Street an' Commercial Street. Public bar, any time after six in the evenin'. If she ain't there by eight, she ain't comin' that night.'

'So, you all just wait there every evening, on the off-chance that this woman will turn up?' Percy enquired sceptically.

'O' course not. We takes it in turns. There's 'alf a dozen of us wot does the work, an' them what doesn't stays in the pub an' keeps a look out. If she comes while some of us is missin', the other gals pass the word on, an' we makes sure we're there on the night when she comes wi' the coach wot's got the dead bubbies in it. Then we collects us shillin's, an' takes one each.'

'So, let me see if I've got this right,' Percy summarised as he glanced down at his notes. 'You all go every night to the Unicorn on the junction of the High Street and Commercial Street, where occasionally this woman turns up between six and eight in the evening. She then leaves word for you to be there on a certain evening and she turns up in a coach in which she's got dead babies, then you take one each, and get paid a shilling to get rid of it. Have I missed anything so far?'

'No — that's pretty much the way o' it. Is that good enough ter stop me an' Tommy takin' the drop?'

'It might be, but I need more information,' Percy advised her. 'What's this woman's name?'

'We just calls 'er Annabelle.'

'What does she look like?'

'She's about forty-five, wi' grey 'air. Yer can't miss 'er, since she's got this gammy eye what looks sideways, like she ain't lookin' at yer proper. That good enough?'

'Probably.' Percy smiled, remembering the description given by Jack and Esther of the sales assistant in 'Timothy's' calling herself "Frances Dickinson", and the lady of the same description who was calling herself "Annabelle Grant" when she ran the adoption agency in Cobham. But there was one additional test he could employ to be sure that Mabel wasn't simply passing on information she'd got from other totties.

'Have you always dealt with this "Annabelle" in the Unicorn? How long has it been going on?'

'In the Unicorn, just a month or two,' Mabel replied. 'Afore that we used ter take a coach down ter this big 'ouse in Surrey, an' collect 'em from there. We used ter get two bob fer us trouble in them days. Then that 'ouse were shut down, on account that fings was gettin' a bit 'ot, an' we was told ter wait until she come ter see us in the Unicorn.'

'And you reckon that this Annabelle's due to pay another visit to the Unicorn, do you?'

'That'd be my best guess,' Mabel confirmed. 'If yer let me out've 'ere, I could let yer know when she comes back, an' when the next delivery o' babies is due.'

'Nice try,' Percy smiled, 'but I'm not as stupid as I look. If we release you from here, you'll disappear into the stews, never to be seen again, and you'll earn yourself ten shillings this time, by tipping off this "Annabelle" woman that we're on to her.'

'I won't — 'onest!' Mabel protested.

Percy shook his head. 'I'll leave word with the Inspector upstairs to have you brought before the beak on a simple robbery charge — you and your accomplice Freestone. But if this all turns out to be a load of horse shit, you'll be back on Attempted Murder, and an appointment with that very efficient Mr Billington at Newgate.'

'I am not dressing up as a prostitute and sitting in a rough public bar every night for God knows how long!' Esther protested as she put her teacup back down heavily on its saucer. They were all, unusually, at Percy and Beattie's house in Hackney on the Saturday following Percy's informative encounter with Mabel Barker in her Shoreditch cell, and they had just swallowed the last of the home-made beefsteak pie. Or almost swallowed, since Beattie's cooking tended to dwell for a while in the oesophagus.

'There has to be a better way,' Jack argued in Esther's defence. 'You can hardly expect her to abandon the children every afternoon and not return until late in the evening, leaving them with Mother, night after night, in the hope that this Annabelle woman will turn up.'

'Do you have a better suggestion?' Percy challenged him. 'You're the only two who can identify "Frances Dickinson", as she's known to you, who's almost certainly the one making the dead baby deliveries.'

'Horrible!' Beattie muttered.

Esther was still in an argumentative mood. 'At the risk of seeming unkind, Uncle Percy, you have no idea what responsibilities and daily duties come with having three infant children. I can't possibly dump them for evenings on end, even though Constance is always so obliging when I need someone to look after them. For the time being, the answer's no, Uncle Percy.'

'How about if you only had to do it for one night?' Jack asked.

Esther gave him the benefit of one of her special 'How did I ever come to marry you?' looks. 'Whose side are you on?'

'Yours, believe it or not,' Jack replied reassuringly. 'Uncle Percy, do I recall what you told us correctly — that this

Dickinson woman comes a few evenings in advance, to alert the totties to when the babies are to be delivered?'

'Of course! We only really need Esther on the evening that the delivery's made.'

'Are you now suggesting,' Esther demanded icily, 'that I collect a dead baby and dump it somewhere?'

'Of course not,' Percy explained. 'You'll move outside with the totties and give the signal to the dozen or so men I'll have waiting in plain clothes in the street. Then you can either allow yourself to be arrested along with the others and I'll rescue you from inside the Shoreditch lock-up, or you slip away with Jack and come back here to Hackney to be reunited with your own very much alive children.'

'Unless Aunt Beattie's fed them by then,' Jack muttered with a grin, only to be slapped across the head by Esther, who was smiling despite herself.

'Jack,' Percy advised him, 'you'll need to sit there posing as a rough workman wiling away the time, keeping a beady eye out for any sign of the lady in question, and then hopefully engaging a totty in conversation for long enough to find out when the delivery's due.'

'And, of course, the fallen woman in question is bound to tell him, isn't she?' Esther added sarcastically.

'Those women will do anything for money,' Jack reassured her.

'That's what I'm concerned about,' Esther complained. 'A few minutes of your boyish charm and they'll be dropping more than information. You're not going in there on your own, do you hear me?'

'Do I hear you volunteering for the escort duties?' Percy grinned.

Esther shook her head. 'No, you don't. You hear me advising you — no, make that *ordering* you — that there's no way my husband is going to spend his evenings in a public bar, drinking himself into a happy mood and being propositioned every five minutes by women of the street.'

Jack looked helplessly across at Percy. 'There must be some other way,' he suggested, and Percy sat deep in thought until Beattie joined them at the table and added her contribution.

'I never imagined I'd ever hear myself suggesting this, but what if Percy were to go with Jack?'

'For what reason?' Percy asked. 'Jack's the one who knows what this woman looks like.'

'Of course, and that's why he has to be there when this woman presents herself,' Beattie reminded him. 'But once he's done that, you can be the one to discover which night the babies are being delivered, can't you?'

Jack looked hopefully at Esther. 'If Uncle Percy comes with me, to preserve my honour, *then* will you let me go?'

Esther laughed ironically. 'The two of you have a terrible record for getting into even more trouble when you're together, but if it means that I don't have to go, then perhaps I'll grit my teeth, pray for a miracle, and agree.'

'And will you also agree to actually be there on the evening of the delivery?' Percy pressed her.

'Do I have a choice?' Esther asked, then sighed with resignation when she saw two heads being shaken.

'Good.' Percy grinned as he sat back in his chair with a look of relief. 'That's settled then. I suggest that we begin tomorrow evening, assuming that I've not been diverted to Highgate.'

'Highgate?' Jack and Esther enquired in unison.

Percy nodded. 'The place where the dead babies are almost certainly coming from. I need to arrange for our Hampstead colleagues to alert us when the letter arrives to advise me that I'm about to become an adoptive father again. A girl this time.'

'At least you won't be able to coax her into the police force,' Esther grumbled as she reached for the teapot.

Chapter Sixteen

'That's right, Billy,' Esther said encouragingly as the lad handed her the correct change in return for her pretended purchase of three cakes costing a penny each.

Nell stood alongside him and politely thanked Esther for her imaginary purchase. 'Can I be the customer next?' she asked eagerly.

Esther smiled. They were a delight to be with and obviously very fond of each other. Esther had no doubt that Billy would lose no time in 'serving' Nell in quite a different sense of that word once they were discharged from the orphanage and sent out into a harsh world in which children's games would be a thing of the past. A lovely idea suddenly came to her and she smiled at Nell's eager face.

'Nell, have you given any thought to what you might like to do for a living when you leave here in October?'

'Not really, Miss,' Nell replied absentmindedly, her eyes glued on Billy's face. 'Perhaps in the scullery of some big 'ouse somewhere.'

'How about more general duties in a smaller house?'

'I 'aven't bin taught cleanin' chimneys yet,' Nell admitted, 'nor black-leadin' fireplaces, neither.'

'Supposing you were to work in a house where they paid you five shillings a week and taught you all the things you still need to learn?'

'Do yer know people like that, Miss?'

'I do indeed,' Esther replied, 'and they've got three beautiful children.'

'Sounds perfect,' Nell said. 'Can yer recommend me to 'em?'

'I can do better than that,' Esther assured her. 'You can meet the man of the house on the day of the Spring Fair.'

'I'd need ter tell Miss Margaret, next time she comes,' Nell advised her, "cos she was talkin' about gettin' me a start at a laundry in Clacton. There might be a job fer Billy there as well, so does this 'ouse yer talkin' about 'ave a job for 'im, d'yer think?'

'I think there's a place down the road where the lady could use the services of a gardener,' Esther replied with a smile, making a mental note to persuade Constance that her garden was looking untidy of late. 'But talking of Miss Margaret, do you know why she's not here today, helping out as usual?'

'We ain't seen 'er since you was last 'ere togevver, Miss,' Nell replied.

Esther felt a pang of guilt and unease. 'But that was almost two weeks ago. I thought she came here several times a week.'

'She normally does,' Nell replied, seemingly unconcerned, 'but we ain't seen 'er since that first time yer was showin' us 'ow ter count money.'

After sending her trainee sales assistants away for their dinner, Esther made her way down to Sister Grace's office with a troubled mind. The last time that Margaret Meacher had been seen at the orphanage to which she was so devoted had been the day when Jack had advised her — rather bluntly, to Esther's mind — that the lady who'd once passed on several unwanted children for transfer to the orphanage had more recently become involved in a trade in dead babies, and Esther had been looking forward to the opportunity to apologise for Jack's almost brutal honesty and assure Margaret that she had nothing to rebuke herself for. She was hoping that Margaret hadn't taken it all the wrong way and taken to hiding herself away from what she most enjoyed — the break in the humdrum routine life of a middle-aged widow that seemed to give her such satisfaction.

'Come in, my dear, and brighten my day by telling me how your lovely and most fortunate of children are faring,' Sister Grace said invitingly as Esther answered the call to enter, following her light knock on the office door.

'They're all very well, thank you,' Esther replied with a worried smile, 'but I'm concerned to hear that Margaret Meacher hasn't been seen here for the best part of two weeks.'

'A little unusual, certainly,' Sister Grace agreed. 'Do you happen to know if she's been unwell?'

'No, but I'm afraid that when I was last here my husband had occasion to give her some rather alarming news regarding the lady who supplied her with those first few orphans she brought here to the orphanage.'

'Yes, I know all about that, dear,' Sister Grace assured her.

Esther's eyebrows rose in surprise. 'You do?'

'Yes. She came back here after having dinner with you and your husband, quite upset to learn that the lady in question appears to have taken to murdering innocent children. She was distressed in case this was the result of her not being able to find any more orphanage places for them, but I reassured her on that score and consoled her with the thought of the lives she'd previously saved by her generous actions. I thought I'd eased her mind, but now I'm beginning to wonder.'

'Could you possibly let me have her home address?'

Sister Grace shook her head. 'If I could, I would, but it's something I've never known, I'm afraid. She never seems to have given it to us, and we didn't like to pry.'

Esther swallowed her disappointment and reverted to singing the praises of Nell and Billy, who'd be making such a splendid difference to the fundraising efforts at the Summer Fayre that was now little over a month away. Then as she joined the queue for the late afternoon country bus back to Barking, darker thought began to trouble her.

Jack had revealed what he knew about the baby farming activities of the lady calling herself Harriet Merchant. Supposing that Margaret had been untruthful regarding how she'd come by those first children she'd delivered to the orphanage? Supposing that Margaret Meacher was a criminal associate of Harriet Merchant, had tipped her off that the police were on to her, and had now gone into hiding herself? It didn't bear thinking about, so Esther tried to banish such thoughts from her troubled mind as she sat back in her swaying, jolting seat and watched the late Spring hedgerows floating past her somewhat grimy bus window.

'So *that* explains what it were about.' Sergeant Carmichael smiled as he listened to what Percy had to tell him in the tea room inside Hampstead Police Station, to which Percy had been directed when enquiring whether any letters had arrived that were addressed to a Mr Percy Jackson. 'Good job we kept it. Just let me finish my tea an' I'll take yer upstairs to dig it out o' my box o' unfiled stuff.'

Ten minutes later, Percy was staring at the neat professional hand that advised him that a girl of six weeks of age would be available for collection two days ago. Cursing himself for not having made enquiries earlier he headed for the nearby railway station, a quick return to the Yard, and an urgent telegram to Jack in Chelmsford. But before that, he left strict instructions with the Station Inspector that a coach and at least four constables should be held in readiness for his urgent instruction with only an hour or two's notice, sometime in the very near future.

Chapter Seventeen

'Things haven't changed much around here,' Jack commented as he stepped carefully over a prostrate drunk while carrying two pint pots over to the table he was sharing with Percy in the rear corner of the public bar of the Unicorn.

'What do you expect?' Percy commented as he blew the froth off his 'Truman's Best'. 'It's pay day — and the ones who didn't go home with their pay packets intact won't dare to once they've had far too many. The beat bobbies will have their hands full dealing with drunken brawls between husbands and wives, and the odds are that we'll be able to add a few murders to the weekly tally by morning.'

'Thank God I got out of here when I did,' Jack muttered as he watched another fight breaking out over near the piano. Hopefully the loser would turn out to be the so-called pianist himself and the piano would be destroyed during the contest. It was part-way there anyway, with half its keys either stuck down by spilt beer or completely missing as the result of past souvenir hunters celebrating a memorable night.

'You don't regret moving to the Detective Branch, then?' Percy said with a smile. 'There are times when I wonder if I did the right thing by you, when you complain so bitterly about your workload.'

'It was fine until I moved to Chelmsford,' Jack explained, 'then I discovered what you must have known for years — that having a supervisory rank brings with it some awful responsibilities. I dread the day that I lose a man in action and have to go and explain it to his widow.'

'I've only had to do it twice,' Percy replied with a downcast look, 'and the second time was worse than the first, since the woman had her kids ranged around her knees and she said to me "How do I explain it to these little people?" I went home with tears in my eyes and kicked down our back fence until Beattie threatened to call the doctor if I didn't leave off.'

'At least we get perks such as this as well,' Jack replied sarcastically. 'Sitting in the middle of a war zone drinking flat beer. Let's hope it pays off in due course, because Esther refuses to believe that we're not actually enjoying ourselves and resents me living back with you in Hackney while we go slumming every night. This is our third evening and I dread to think how much paper's piled up on my desk in Chelmsford while we sit here feeding the brewery's profits.'

'Do you think you'll stay there, or do you hanker for a return to The Yard?'

'Obviously I preferred working with you all the time, but I have to think of Esther and the kids, particularly since there's another one due in September. At present, we have a big house, a decent garden, fresh country air, a school for Lily that's not crammed with apprentice hooligans, and all the benefits of a crime-free local community. If we came back to London, we'd lose most of that, so I just have to grit my teeth and get on with it.'

'You didn't mention the advantage of being so close to your mother,' Percy remarked with heavy sarcasm as he looked past Jack to where four burly constables called in by the landlord were settling the fight democratically by bashing every head with their billy clubs.

'Thank God Mother and Esther seem to get on well enough, to the point of ganging up on me sometimes.'

'It's good for Esther to have an older woman around,' Percy observed from his standpoint of total ignorance on the subject, 'since she can look to her for advice.'

'Advice that most of the time she politely ignores. Take the matter of domestic help, for example. Esther's so damned proud that she won't even consider bringing in some local woman to help with the cleaning. Most days she's totally exhausted when I get home, and that makes her grumpy. And it's not just me who bears the brunt of that — some days poor old Lily and Bertie hardly dare open their mouths in case they say something that starts her off.'

'Perhaps we're better off being the bread winners,' Percy grinned. 'At least we don't have to earn our money a shilling at a time, up an alley with some smelly drunk, like those four over there on the table behind you. My guess is that they're waiting for this "Annabelle" woman.'

'Let's hope so,' Jack replied. 'I never thought the day would come when I tired of sitting in a pub with you, but that day arrived yesterday. Nothing personal.'

'Talking of matters personal,' Percy smiled, 'take a casual look behind you and tell me which of those totties you most fancy.'

Jack turned around on his stool to look at the quartet of women at the table behind them, then looked away quickly when one of them gave him a cheery wave and a gap-toothed smile.

'Hang on,' Percy hissed. 'There's a woman just come in who may well be our "Annabelle". She fits the description anyway.'

Jack swivelled, looked briefly at the familiar face, then turned away. 'That's her. I just hope she didn't notice me.'

'She wasn't even looking in your direction,' Percy replied, 'more's the pity. I can lip-read pretty well when the person's facing me, and I got enough of it to confirm that she's giving them a time and a day. The problem is that I couldn't make out the day and now she's off outside again.'

'At least we got half of the story,' Jack told Percy as they resumed their pints, 'so can we go home now?'

'What's the point, when we don't know the precise day?'

Jack shrugged. 'Esther and I will just have to come back here every night.'

'There might be a better way,' Percy replied with the sort of sneaky grin that Jack knew well, and which never meant anything good for him. 'Just wait here a minute,' Percy added as he rose and walked outside.

A few minutes elapsed, during which Jack was asking himself what the Devil his uncle was up to this time. Then some instinct made him turn around in time to see Percy with a lascivious grin on his face, chatting to one of the women. When Percy returned and swallowed the remains of his pint, Jack was both suspicious and somewhat outraged.

'You didn't have to enjoy yourself to the extent of ingratiating yourself with a totty, and if you promise that we can leave now I won't tell Aunt Beattie.'

'And I won't tell Esther,' Percy grinned in reply, just as a light hand fell on Jack's shoulder and he caught the faint whiff of second-hand stout. He turned and there was the woman, grinning down at him.

'Yer Dad told us as 'ow it's yer burfday, an' yer've never 'ad it afore, so if yer'd care ter come wi' me, I'll introduce yer ter the delights yer'll find up a lady's petticoats.'

Jack shot a furious glare at a grinning Percy and came out with the first excuse he could think of. 'I don't have any money, I'm afraid.'

''S alright, dearie, yer Dad give us the shillin', so up yer gets.'

Jack looked back at Percy for some prospect of rescue, but Percy simply grinned back at him. 'Off yer go, son,' he encouraged him in his best labourer's voice, 'never look a gift 'orse in the mouf, an gi' 'er one fer me!'

A totally bewildered and horrified Jack allowed himself to be led outside by the large woman, who advised him as they reached the front door that, 'Me name's Gertie, an' it's just up 'ere.'

In the grip of what felt like a surreal nightmare, Jack was led up a dark alleyway to the side of the pub, then down a long ramp that seemed to be leading towards a fence. When they reached it, Gertie lifted up a strand of loose wire and ducked under it, holding out her hand for Jack to follow. Hand in cold sweaty hand they made their way carefully down a stony embankment towards a set of railway carriages that sat in a siding, where Gertie threw open an unlocked door.

'In yer gets, darlin',' she encouraged him as she went in ahead of him, then turned and lifted her skirts and petticoats in a skilful and much-practised sweep that revealed a total absence of any restricting undergarments. Once Jack was inside the carriage with the door closed, she sat back on one of the padded bench seats and opened her legs.

What might have happened next remained a matter of conjecture as the carriage door was thrown open again, to reveal a uniformed constable.

'Gotcha!' he smiled. 'Yer under arrest fer tottin', so back on yer feet.'

'I ain't done nuffin!' Gertie protested.

'Only 'cos I stopped yer,' she was reminded by the constable.

'This is a disgrace, keepin' an 'onest girl from earnin' a few bob on the side.'

'On yer back, yer mean,' the constable grinned as he gestured for her to step out of the carriage, where she was outraged to see a smiling Percy waiting for her with his police badge held high in the air.

'Detective Inspector Enright, Scotland Yard,' he managed before he was drowned out by a tirade of foul-mouthed obscenities whose general drift was to the effect that he would be better off pursuing real criminals. He smiled at the constable. 'Such a lady. Take her to Commercial Street and put her in an interview room. One without a window and only one chair. I'll not be long behind you. Charge her with railway trespass and prostitution — for the time being, anyway.'

'Trespass ain't a criminal matter,' Gertie reminded him.

Percy smiled. 'Take out "railway trespass" and insert "accessory after the fact to infanticide", if you'd be so obliging.'

'What's that when it's 'ome?' Gertie demanded.

Percy smiled as he stepped to one side to allow the constable to grab her arm and force her back up the slope. 'Being a party to the murder of innocent babies,' he advised her, and her ongoing protests at the injustice of this new charge were audible long after she'd disappeared through the light mist that was beginning to form as the late evening became the early morning.

'Thank you for rescuing me when you did,' Jack said. 'I'm not sure how long I could have kept it up.'

'An unfortunate choice of words, in the circumstances,' Percy replied. 'And you owe me a shilling, by the way.'

'That's nothing to what you owe me!' Jack protested. 'What was that all about, anyway?'

'We now have a totty in custody, fearful that she's about to be charged with an offence which, for all she knows, carries the death penalty, who can actually advise us of the date of "Annabelle's" return.'

'But she'll tip Annabelle off, won't she?' Jack objected.

Percy grinned again. 'Aren't you rather assuming that she'll be released in time to do so?'

Thirty minutes later Percy was smiling his way through the screamed abuse from the woman standing in the corner of the interview room being firmly held by a constable.

'Yer set me up, yer rotten bleedin' bastard! That weren't yer son at all, were it?'

'Would you have believed me if I'd told you he was my nephew?'

'An' wot were all that about murderin' bubbies? Yer gotta be jokin', right?'

'Wrong. You were visited this evening by a woman you know only as "Annabelle", who was giving you the date for the next delivery of dead babies. Where were you planning on dumping this one? The same railway carriage where you almost gave my nephew a nasty dose of the pox?'

'I'm clean, I'll 'ave yer know,' Gertie countered, 'but if the bubbies are dead when we get 'em, 'ow can yer charge me wi' murder? That can't be right, can it?'

'Let's hope you have a good lawyer who can persuade a jury of that,' Percy replied with more confidence than he felt. 'But good lawyers cost money, do they not? And I'd hazard a guess that you're only worth what you earned last night, unless you pissed that away already.'

'Yer bastard,' Gertie growled. 'I s'pose this is all a come-on till I give yer what yer wantin', like all the others. D'yer wanna do it 'ere, or down in some cell somewhere?'

'It's no come on, I can assure you,' Percy replied with a downturn of his lips, 'and I'd no more have sexual intercourse with you than I'd put my Hampton in a meat press. But if you want to avoid the Murder charge, you can co-operate in another way.'

'What yer wantin', then?'

'The day and time of Annabelle's next delivery of dead babies.'

'Sunday, at seven in the evenin'.'

'Excellent. See, it wasn't too difficult, was it? From now until Monday morning you'll be down in one of the cells in this poorly equipped establishment.'

'Yer a bastard, yer know that, don't yer?'

'So I've been advised, more than once. And by better than you. Take her down constable.'

'Never let it be said that Jackson Enright doesn't know how to show a girl a good time,' Esther hissed as she sipped her glass of lemonade and stared out disapprovingly at the motley company of prostitutes and drunks from the corner of the public bar of The Unicorn that Jack and Percy had occupied only two evenings previously. 'First of all he gets me pregnant for the fourth time, then he abandons the three existing children at the home of his aunt and uncle and brings me into one of the lowest pubs that the East End has to offer — and *that's* saying something — and forces me to watch women touting for custom while drunken men stagger around the place narrowly avoiding each other, then issuing challenges to fight when they collide.'

'At least we avoided Sunday dinner at Mother's,' Jack offered by way of consolation, earning a snort this time.

'Boring though that usually is, at least those assembled round the table are sober and smelling as if they washed some time during the previous week. And I doubt very much whether she swallowed our excuse about coming down to Percy's to advise him on how to string up tomato plants.'

'At least it'll only be for the one occasion.'

'You hope. You haven't explained where Percy's got to and what's supposed to happen once the carriage full of dead babies arrives.'

'Shh!' Jack warned her with an apprehensive glance at the table behind them, which contained the same women as the last time he'd been here. He caught one of them staring at him and looked hastily away as his face went red at the mere memory of the circumstances in which he'd left the place last time. 'We know what we have to do,' he reminded Esther. 'As soon as that woman "Annabelle" appears, and the girls follow her outside, you slide in behind them to make it look as if you're one of the company, then wave your bonnet in the air to alert the bobbies who'll be waiting to pounce. Uncle Percy's presumably out there, organising it all and waiting to order the arrests.'

If he'd expected Esther to be satisfied with this explanation, he was about to be disappointed.

'How can I possibly hope to carry off the pretence of being a working woman when I'm so obviously pregnant?' she demanded. 'I look about as attractive as one of those cows you see grazing on the far side of the railway line at home.'

'Some men are strangely attracted to women who look like that,' Jack assured her.

Esther glared at him. 'How come you know so much about these women and their clients?' she demanded, just as one of the ladies who answered that description got up from the table behind them and plonked herself down on Jack's knee, throwing one gaudily dressed arm around his neck.

''Allo again, darlin'. 'Ow d'yer go wi' Gertie the other night? We ain't seen 'er since you an' 'er set off fer the railway carriage.'

'You must be mistaking me for someone else,' Jack muttered, red-faced, as he lowered his head.

'Not me,' the woman insisted. 'Yer were wi' yer Dad, it were yer birfday, an' yer Dad bought yer a present. I never forgets a nice lookin' boy like you.'

'May I take it that my husband engaged one of your friends in the line of business?' Esther demanded, her face growing paler the angrier she got. 'Your business, that is — not his.'

'Leave it alone Esther, please,' Jack pleaded with her. 'It's easily explained.'

'Sure, it's easy explained,' the woman replied, smiling unpleasantly at Esther. 'Yer obviously up the duff an' I bet yer man 'ere's not gettin' it no more, so 'e comes ter one've us fer 'is simple needs. Yer wanna keep yer man? Make sure yer opens yer legs more often.'

'How dare you, you — you cheap — you... ' Esther spluttered, but to Jack's intense relief they heard one of the other women calling their friend back to their table, just as the older lady who'd once sold them baby clothes in an Oxford Street store could be seen in the doorway that led back out into the street, beckoning them outside.

'We'll discuss this later,' Esther spat at Jack as she rose from their table and tagged along behind the other women, who had all risen to leave. Outside was a coach with a bored looking coachman seated on the front board and "Annabelle" was in the process of opening the side door to reveal a small collection of carpet bags as Esther reached the front door and raised her hat high in the air, waving it from side to side for good measure.

A dozen police whistles sounded all at once and uniformed constables appeared from all points of the compass, surrounding the coach and attaching handcuffs to two of the women, who were already reaching inside the vehicle for one of the bags. Esther shouted and pointed to 'Annabelle' when it seemed that she might evade capture as she strode swiftly away up Commercial Street. When no-one responded, Jack raced after her, brought her to the ground with a full body tackle, then reached into his jacket pocket for a set of hand restraints and cuffed her wrists behind her back, before calling to two constables to add her to the collection of women already in the process of being loaded into the back of a Black Maria.

As Jack walked back towards the chaos he was approached by a uniformed Inspector who appeared to be in overall supervision of the operation. 'Sergeant Enright?' the Inspector enquired.

'That's me.

'I'm Inspector Dalgleish, from the local mob. Yeir uncle sends his compliments, and his apologies fer bein' obliged tae miss all the fun.'

'Unusual for him,' Jack observed. 'Where is he, exactly?'

'On his way tae Highgate by now, I'd imagine.'

As soon as the action had begun outside The Unicorn, one uniformed officer had been detailed to run back to Commercial Street Police Station and alert the desk sergeant, who had then made a prearranged telephone call to Hampstead to advise Percy Enright and his team that the second part of the carefully co-ordinated operation might be commenced.

Four police coaches clattered to a halt outside the nursing home in Highgate and eight uniformed officers were led down the front drive by Percy, who instructed most of them to form a semicircle outside the front door, while several more were detailed to cover any side or rear entrances that might exist. Percy hammered on the door and when a uniformed 'nurse' opened it, she was bowled over backwards by the force of the officers rushing in and spreading out throughout the interior of the building. Percy made straight for the Matron's office and flung open the door.

A startled 'Matron Merchant' rose from her desk with a faintly outraged look. 'You obviously received our letter, Mr Jackson, but this late hour in the evening is hardly...' She stopped mid-sentence as she saw the police badge raised high in the air and the two uniformed constables filling the doorway behind Percy.

'My gleeful apologies for the earlier deception. In real life I'm Detective Inspector Percy Enright, and you're under arrest.'

'On what charge?'

'Mass murder will do for a start. Your evil little business is at an end.'

'I was merely protecting other children from what I had to endure.'

'You can pluck at my heartstrings back at the police station. Buckle her please, gentlemen. If she struggles, be as rough as you like.'

Chapter Eighteen

'We've got your partner in crime safely locked up in Shoreditch,' Percy told the woman seated in front of him, wrists still manacled. 'We also have several of your intended delivery girls, your coachman, and five dead babies. I'd say that whatever lies you're planning to tell me will be falling on deaf ears. You're heading for the hangman, whatever your name is.'

The woman calling herself 'Matron Merchant' smiled at him with apparent unconcern. 'Do you think I don't know that, Inspector? At the moment the only thing causing me the slightest discomfort are these awful restraints around my wrists. If you'd give the order for them to be removed, I'll tell you not only what you want to know, but many things that you almost certainly *don't* want to learn.'

Percy nodded to the constable standing by the door and he moved forward and unlocked the restraints.

The woman rubbed her wrists briefly, then looked back up at Percy. 'Where do you wish me to start?'

'I usually find that the beginning is a good place,' Percy replied with faint sarcasm, 'so why not treat me to that?'

'I take it that we have the entire night to spare?'

'I certainly have, but you'll find that you have much more free time, now that you'll be staring at four walls for several months, before a noose is placed round your neck.'

'You have a kindly face,' Harriet observed without any obvious concern, 'and so I can only assume that the words that you intended to be cruel were in fact part of your performance with all prisoners.'

'Not entirely,' Percy replied as his face hardened. 'I was just thinking of all those dead babies.'

'And what about the ones who lived?' she countered. 'The dozens and dozens who were saved from the life that I, and others like me, endured as orphans? Believe me, the ones who died were spared something far worse than death.'

'I cannot bring myself to understand,' Percy replied, 'how someone who obviously has a background in nursing could bring themselves to kill an innocent infant.'

'My real name is Harriet Crouch,' she began. 'I say "real", but I'm referring to the name they gave me in the orphanage to which I was first consigned — one of several. I never knew my real parents, or my true name, and I have no idea what misfortune led to my first memory being of a stern lady throwing water in my face. I must have been about two years old, by my calculation, and presumably it was what turned out to be one of the few occasions when I was allowed to wash. I also recall the pain of having my ankles firmly manacled to a concrete floor after I'd wandered too close to the tall front gate of this dreadful place, then being beaten severely when I cried several hours later.'

'"Cruelty begets cruelty", is that going to be your defence?'

Harriet shook her head. 'I am not constructing any defence, Inspector. I fully intend to plead guilty to those acts I've performed. I am, on this occasion, placing you in possession of facts that have been ignored by everyone I have sought to relate them to since my first escape from human bondage at the age of twelve. You will learn in due course, when you examine your records, that as "Harriet Crouch" I had several confrontations with the law. Always for stealing, and never for prostitution, which seems to have become the chosen lifestyle of many who endured what I did. May I continue?'

When Percy nodded, she looked blankly up at the ceiling and resumed her story.

'My second institution for the blamelessly orphaned was somewhere near the river — Deptford, I believe it to have been. I was sent there as a punishment because I, along with several others, had stolen food. The food we were supposed to be given to eat was rudimentary enough — gruel, stale black bread, and some sort of bean mash — but we were never given enough of it, and there was a belief that the woman in charge of the orphanage was selling it to hawkers on the street. Whatever the truth of it, a few of us took to stealing it, and found ourselves behind the grim walls of this prison of sorts, where we soon learned what it is to be female and dependent for one's very existence on men.'

'Sexual exploitation?' Percy enquired, now paying more serious attention to what he was hearing.

'Daily,' Harriet replied through tightened lips. 'In fact, to be more precise, hourly. This place to which we "out of control" girls had been consigned was called an orphanage, but it was in reality a prison, staffed by men who had slipped well under the parapet of decent behaviour. Depraved monsters who were prepared to work for a mere pittance in exchange for their keep and the endless opportunities that were afforded to them to explore young bodies with their filthy tastes. There were some young boys there also, and they seemed to suffer a similar fate. But in the main it was young girls, and if you can believe it, we were taught that this was our punishment for being a burden on society — for having the bare-faced audacity to live, as a ragged reminder that underneath your stern-faced hypocritical Christian facade there is unmet poverty, disease, neglect, vice and squalor.'

'I worked for many years in the East End,' Percy advised her, 'so I've seen something of that, believe me.'

'You've seen *nothing*!' Harriet spat back at him, her eyes narrowed in anger. 'You see only what you want to see — you and others in authority. You see only the consequences and do nothing about their causes. The countless women, and not just those consigned to orphanages, brought up to obey men without question, or risk a beating. Women condemned to endless childbirth — for which their men blame them before seeking the solace of other women — giving birth in conditions that we would condemn in farm outbuildings, then somehow trying to keep their own body and soul together while raising children alone, their fathers having long abandoned them. Little wonder that they resort to prostitution, and even less wonder that they put their daughters, and sometimes their sons, to the same disgusting trade. No-one cares about them, provided that they're not in evidence when the Queen, or one of her pampered brood, is out in their carriage, waving at their loyal subjects and proudly displaying their offspring as a living moral example of how children should be raised.'

'At least those women do their utmost to preserve the lives of their children,' Percy observed sourly. 'They don't kill them off and leave them inside railways carriages, in cardboard boxes, or in the Thames.'

'Do they not?' Harriet challenged him. 'Do you think that every dead child you've come across in your trade is the result of my actions? Have you any idea how many children die at birth naturally, because of the conditions in which they're born, or because their mother is too malnourished to have any milk in her breast to feed it? Can you even begin to imagine what it must be like for a heartbroken mother to nurse a child to its breast, if only to stop it screaming from starvation, and then watch it slowly die an uncomprehending death? Can you? *Can you?*'

As she banged the table with both fists, the constable moved forward to restrain her, but Percy raised his hand in the air.

'Leave her be. She has every right to be angry. But no right to take infant lives, so tell me, madam, how you went from being an abused orphan yourself to organising the deaths of others.'

'I didn't set out to,' Harriet replied as she wiped a tear of rage from her cheek. 'Like everyone else who grew up in that filthy place, I believed that it was my lot in life simply to be used as a depository for men's lust. A sack of potatoes to be taken off the shelf and pounded. Left sore and bleeding, with a kick or a punch if I cried out too loudly. Then I discovered that it was not just me; that every other child in that hellhole was suffering the same thing. So, we planned our escape. Three of us; you've met one of them, I believe?'

'Annabelle Grant — or is it Frances Dickinson?' Percy asked.

Harriet smiled grimly. 'Even she chose to change her name. In the so-called orphanage she was known as "Amy Jackson", and she kept that name for some time. The third one who escaped was called Sadie Brown, but she changed her name to Harriet Bradbury, out of some sort of respect for me, when I led the escape party of three out of that free brothel. She returned later to set fire to the place, then came out of the long sentence she incurred for that already addicted to opium. Does that shock you — that people in prison have access to drugs? You'd be even more shocked if you knew what they had to do to get it from the screws who staff those places.'

'I already knew about her, although I wasn't aware of her connection with you,' Percy advised her. 'Where is she now?'

Harriet laughed bitterly. 'In a pauper's grave down near the river. They found her body in a gutter in Limehouse with a chest-full of the opium that she'd been supplying for the Chinamen who killed her when she was robbed of the money she was supposed to have collected for them on the street. Just another "fallen woman" found in "unfortunate circumstances", according to a Coroner who was no doubt anxious to earn his fee and begin his dinner.'

'So, you and Amy Jackson — along with this third woman — escaped from the orphanage, you say? How did you manage that, exactly?'

Harriet grimaced. 'We made use of the life skills we'd already been taught. We were free meat to the men, and sometimes the women, who ran the orphanage, but the tradesmen who came and went could only ogle us from a distance and fantasise what it would be like to violate our slowly forming bodies. So, we let it be known to the man who collected the offal from the kitchen that we'd be happy to turn his fantasies into reality in exchange for a safe passage out of there under a week's supply of rotting filth. Once we were clear of the place, we ran as hard as we could until we were in Thames Street, hiding between cotton bales and stealing food from the rats on the wharves. It was still better than we'd been used to.'

'And then?'

'Then it seemed as if Amy and I had been rescued by Fate. We learned of a convent in Hoxton, attached to a priory, and it was easy to break in there regularly and steal food. One night we were caught, though, and brought before a stern-faced abbess who gave us a choice between joining the convent or being handed over to the constables. So, we both took the veil; as you can readily imagine, a vow of poverty meant nothing to two girls who'd been competing with rats for food, and as for chastity — believe me, we *prayed* for it, after what we'd experienced at the hands of men. However, we both experienced some difficulty with the vow of obedience.'

'You became *nuns*?' Percy enquired disbelievingly.

Harriet shook her head. 'We were both only novices when we slipped away one night. By then we'd become young women, and had been educated, but we made a solemn vow to each other that we'd remain loyal and that whenever one of us was in need, the other would come to her aid. We went our separate ways, but I'd made a new friend. The nun who supervised the novices was little older than me and she'd sort of taken me under her wing. She knew of a local paupers' hospital — more of an asylum and workhouse, really — in Whitechapel, where they were in constant need of women to tend the sick and dying, and she'd mentioned that I might perhaps find some sort of work there one day. So, I chose to bring that day forward and for ten years I worked there and learned the skills of a midwife to the impoverished wretches who drifted in there in the last extremities of childbirth, before being cast out again clutching their starving babies.'

'You should contact Mr Dickens,' Percy said quietly, 'since you seem to have enough here for another of his stories.'

'The difference being that I've lived it, while Charles Dickens simply writes about it and makes a living out of selling his books full of other peoples' misery. I was there for ten years or so, during which time I kept in contact with Amy Jackson, who against all the odds had met a man, accepted his offer of marriage and was living in a place called Braintree, in Essex.'

'I know of it,' Percy advised her. 'So she at least had survived all the hardship?'

'Yes and no. Her husband was a brewer's labourer too fond of the product that he helped to make. He took to beating her by way of daily exercise, then threw her out when she became pregnant. She came looking for me in her desperation and I smuggled her into my tiny room at the asylum, along with the baby, which in due course died. It was a boy and his was the first body that we got rid of, and by that process we learned how easy it was.'

'There were others, obviously,' Percy observed unnecessarily.

Harriet nodded. 'Yes, but not until some years later, when I began finding homes for most of those that came my way.'

'And how did that come about?'

'Well, when Amy lost her baby, she was devastated and was determined to either have another of her own or adopt one. Where I worked at the asylum there was no shortage of unwanted babies, so Amy took one for herself — a girl — and went back to Braintree to start a new life when she heard that her former husband had died in a fight. The next I heard from her was an excited letter telling me that she'd been in the local market, selling vegetables for a farmer and his wife who'd taken her in as a domestic, when she was certain that she'd caught sight of our old novice mistress from our convent days. She was still calling herself "Sister Grace" but was now running an orphanage for her Order in Brentwood. So, under a false name, Amy approached the orphanage on the pretence of seeking a buyer for her employer's market garden produce. She called herself "Annabelle Grant", to eliminate any possibility that this Sister Grace would remember her.'

'She's the same woman we arrested earlier this evening in Shoreditch?'

'Yes, that's right — she's actually Amy Jackson. "Grant" was her married name, and she chose "Annabelle" because she liked it.'

'Why didn't she want this Sister Grace to remember her?'

'That's easy to explain. Like me, she was embarrassed that we'd slipped out of the convent while still under vows, without telling anyone and without seeking absolution. But when she explained to me how well the orphans were being treated at the Holy Heart, we made it our life's work to steer other waifs and strays in their direction, using a woman who ran the local post office in Braintree as the deliverer. I don't think Sister Grace ever cottoned on to the fact that the orphans were being supplied by two women who had once been training for holy orders under her supervision.'

'You were *both* supplying these children?' Percy asked.

Harriet nodded. 'Correct. Amy was rounding up all those who she came across in Essex, and I was bringing unwanted babies from the asylum in London.'

'So how did it change from live orphans to dead babies?'

Harriet frowned. 'The orphanage in Brentwood soon ran out of places. Too many unwanted babies and not enough bed spaces. You won't believe me, I know, but we tried every orphanage we could find within fifty miles of London, until we'd filled every last one to capacity. Then we hit on the idea of offering them for adoption, and Amy moved down to Surrey — to be as far away as possible from anyone who might know her from her days in London and Essex — and rented a large house from which she could conduct a legitimate adoption agency. I worked with her for the first year or so, delivering babies for girls who needed midwifery services but didn't necessarily want to keep their babies, and we soon had a thriving trade in adoptions. In the hope of expanding our market — particularly for adoptions — I sank every penny we'd earned that far into the first three months' lease on those premises in Highgate to which you came, posing as a potential adopter. You were very convincing, by the way.'

'I was once actually in that position,' Percy explained. 'But you're avoiding the crimes that landed you in here.'

'You call them crimes, of course, because you're paid to uphold and protect this rotten society that we pride ourselves on so much. But I ask you to consider what sort of lives might have been led by those helpless infants had they lived. The same as the ones we'd led? Used, abused, despised, exploited, outcast, starving wretches?'

'You set yourselves up as God, and chose those babies that were to be adopted, and those that were to die,' Percy argued as his face set in anger.

'*We* didn't — society did,' Harriet countered. 'Believe me, every child we could find a home for was adopted.'

'At considerable personal profit for yourselves.'

'When you examine the books of my Highgate enterprise, as I'm sure you will, you'll see that every penny that came in was expended on securing a future for more children. The problem was that there were more abandoned children than there were couples seeking to adopt. Some of the children died through natural starvation in the early days, when we could barely afford to feed ourselves, let alone the infants in our care, but towards the end we resorted to laudanum or morphine. I cried bitter tears for every single one, although I don't expect you to believe that.'

'But your high moral principles didn't prevent you from hiring prostitutes to dispose of the corpses,' Percy pointed out.

'What would you have suggested, in our situation — report the deaths to the authorities, have our houses of mercy closed down, and condemn more innocent children to what we'd had to endure?'

'I don't know what I find the more sickening,' Percy said as he rose to leave, 'the pretended moral justification for running a profitable business out of other people's misery, or the bare-faced lack of remorse.'

'Why should I be remorseful for saving other poor souls from going through what I went through? And what is the more moral — maintaining a hypocritical regime that on its surface preserves a blameless Christian society which turns a blind eye to the squalor and hopeless desperation of those trodden under its self-satisfied feet, or defying the law and minimising the misery of others?'

'You'll find that playing the Angel of Mercy won't save you from the gallows.'

'I welcome the gallows, Inspector. I have no life left to regret losing and any temporary suffering as the noose tightens around my throat will be as nothing compared with the memories of what I've lived through.'

'See that she's fed, then well guarded,' Percy instructed the constable as he walked out of the room with a white face.

The sun was just rising in the east when Beattie drew back the bedroom curtains and saw Percy standing motionless in their back garden. She threw her housecoat over her nightdress, hurried downstairs and ran bare-foot onto the lawn, reaching his side and looking, horror-stricken, at his blank face.

'What happened, did you forget your key? Have you been out here all night? Why didn't you throw something up at my window?'

When none of these questions met with any response, she put her hand on his arm, only to have it shaken off angrily. She stepped round in front of him, and stared, horror-stricken, at the red streaks left by burning tears. 'What's the matter, Percy? What's happened? Jack told me that his half of the operation went well — was there a problem with yours?'

'Not until I spoke with our prisoner,' Percy rasped by way of reply. 'Then I realised something. I've spent all my working years supporting a rotten, sick, stinking system that calls itself a civilised society, yet treats its weakest members with a cruelty that not even animals sink to. And I've earned money — a reasonable amount of it — in the process. I'm as bad as they are. I hate being a police officer, I'm ashamed of being a police officer, and I intend to resign at the earliest opportunity, while I still possess a soul.'

'I'll make some tea,' Beattie offered, and walked sadly away, hoping that Jack was already awake.

Chapter Nineteen

Jack walked carefully across the lawn carrying two mugs of steaming hot tea, while Beattie looked fearfully out through the kitchen window and Esther paused to gaze down on them from the spare bedroom, after lifting Miriam from her makeshift cot.

Jack held one of the mugs under Percy's nose as his uncle stood with his back to him, staring fixedly into the flower bed.

'It wouldn't fit,' Jack murmured.

After a moment Percy looked back at him. 'Pardon?'

'It wouldn't fit.'

'*What* wouldn't fit *where?*'

'This mug of tea, where you're about to tell me to shove it. Best drink it.'

Percy allowed himself a grim smile. 'I assume that your Aunt Beattie sent you out here to talk some sense into me?'

'No, she knows from bitter experience that I never talk sense,' Jack joked. 'I came out on my own accord, since breakfast's nearly ready and I need to mask my greed behind someone who can eat more sausages than me.'

'Did she tell you that I'm going to resign from the force?'

'No, she said that you were thinking of it. That's why I mentioned sausages.'

'What on earth have sausages got to do with my resignation?'

'They both smell better than they taste.'

'Meaning?'

'Meaning that you'd miss it, and regret having made a hasty decision.'

'Did you interview Annabelle Grant?'

'No, I thought I'd leave that to you. We're going home this morning. How did you go with Harriet Merchant?'

'Her real name's "Harriet Crouch", and after hearing her story I realised that I've wasted my life defending and upholding a system that's rotten to the core.'

'Come on, Uncle,' Jack protested lightly, 'the Met has its flaws, I'll grant you, but that's a bit harsh.'

'Not just the Met — society as a whole.'

'The very society that you've devoted your entire career to protecting?'

Percy swung round angrily to confront Jack, who was still holding two mugs of tea, occasionally taking sips from one of them.

'Yes — *that* society. The proud British Empire, ruled over by a fat Queen who hides behind her long-extended grief at the loss of her husband, when there are thousands in London alone who grieve for babies they've lost, whose lives have been ruined by the animal brutality that masks its true nature behind a facade of Christian piety. A nation of grasping, hypocritical arseholes who're content to take advantage — financial, social and sexual — of those weaker than themselves. People who look to them for the charity that they purport to extend, while all the while these pillars of moral rectitude are seeking more ways of exploiting the positions of authority and privilege that they've done nothing to earn except to be born in the right place to the right family. I've been helping them maintain all that and taking money for it all these years. I'm even worse than they are, in some ways, and it's high time that I threw it in and took to earning an honest living.'

Jack fell silent for a moment while searching for the means to get back into the conversation, then inspiration dawned. 'Just a few feet from where we're standing are some garden chairs,' he reminded Percy. 'I remember a brash, naive young man who even at seventeen was not fit to be let out without a responsible adult by his side. He was seated next to a mature, caring man who he idolised, and he was asking all about becoming a police officer. I can still remember what that man told me.'

There was no immediate response, so he continued. 'He told me that it was the most noble profession a young man could consider. A profession dedicated to preserving the weak from the strong, the good from the evil. A means of ensuring that we were not condemned to live like animals in the jungle, where the mighty eat the feeble. That a well organised and properly ordered society was our only hope, and that within it the word of God might clearly be heard. Are you telling me, over ten years later, that this was all rubbish, that you never meant a word of it, and that you were cynically committing me to a wasted life?'

'Clever use of words, Jack, not to mention a powerful argument. I obviously taught you too well.'

'You taught me everything I know, Uncle Percy,' Jack persevered as he felt tears rising, 'and thanks to you I can now hold my head up and be proud of what I've become. Thanks to the career I chose with your guidance I'm now married to the most beautiful woman I've ever known, with three gorgeous children and another one on the way, living in a fine house in the country, and with prospects of further advancement. *You* may be ashamed of what we do for a living, but I'm not, and right now I'm about to go back inside and eat your sausages.'

'You wouldn't dare.'

'Would I not? Am I not one of those you now seem to despise? Those who pretend to be the guardians of the only way of life we know, imperfect though it is? Why would I not take the food from the mouth of the very man who raised me from a stupid boy to someone who now feels proud every time he walks into Chelmsford Police Station? Someone who's even more proud to claim Inspector Enright as his uncle? I'm a copper, after all, and we're all corrupt and greedy. Race you to the sausages.'

'I'm still intending to resign, Jack, but I can't do that on an empty stomach.'

Esther smiled encouragingly from two paces behind the stall, while Nell extolled the virtues of the strawberry flan that the local blacksmith's wife was considering buying, and Billy was giving Mrs Barton her correct change for the purchase of two mince pies. It was the day of the Summer Fayre and sales were brisk. Jack was talking to Uncle Percy, while Aunt Beattie was hovering in the background with her purse open, looking hopeful.

There was a brief lull, during which Esther sidled up to Nell.

'You remember I mentioned, when we were rehearsing for today, that you'd meet a man who might be interested in engaging you as a domestic in his big house in Barking?'

'Yes, of course,' Nell replied eagerly.

'Well, that's him over there, standing with the older man and woman. He's the younger looking one in the brown hat.'

'He's lovely!' Nell murmured, but before Esther could experience any doubt about what she had in mind, Nell added, 'But not as lovely as Billy. He's doing well, isn't he?'

'He certainly is,' Esther agreed as the family group walked towards them. Jack detached himself from Percy and Beattie and walked round the back of the stall, giving Esther a loving kiss on the lips and patting her eight-month-old bulge.

As Percy and Beattie reached the stall, Jack whispered in Esther's ear, 'Let Uncle Percy buy whatever he fancies. He's taking full advantage of Beattie's campaign to prevent him from resigning, and you're about to see him embarking on a world record bid for cake consumption.'

'Do you think he really will resign?' Esther asked.

Jack smiled. 'I doubt it. Harriet Crouch and Amy Jackson look like escaping a hanging, after he talked the Treasury Counsel into letting him be a witness and argue for clemency, and I think he's regained some of his faith in the system. Oh dear, here comes Mother; I'd better head her off.' He wandered back out onto the crowded church lawn, and before moving back to her sales position Nell looked sideways at Esther with a look of concern.

'That *was* the man who might be hiring me as a domestic, wasn't it?'

'That's right,' Esther confirmed, 'the one you said was lovely.'

'You obviously think so too,' Nell replied in a concerned voice, 'since you let him take liberties with you.'

'Why wouldn't I?' Esther replied with a grin, 'Since he's my husband?'

Nell took that information in for a moment, then her face broke into a broad smile. 'So I'd be working for *you*?'

'Of course. I hear that good domestics are hard to come by these days, so I thought I'd take my pick of the best while I could. We have a spare room, so you could live in, and everyone's forever telling me that I'm too proud to allow anyone else to clean my house, so this way I can accommodate everyone's wishes. I take it that five shillings a week would be reasonable, if you're living in? I'm afraid I don't know much about these things.'

'That would be wonderful!' Nell replied happily as she squeezed Esther's arm. Then her face fell slightly. 'But you don't have anything for Billy?'

'I've even thought of that,' Esther smiled. 'I saw him scything the lawn at the "Holy Heart", and I've already found two people who would be prepared to pay a shilling each for the same excellent service. You're actually standing on one of the lawns that he'll be scything, and the vicar has agreed to let him live in that groundsman's cottage that hasn't seen a groundsman for years. I think the vicar's a bit embarrassed at his own feeble efforts, to tell you the truth.'

'You mentioned two lawns,' Nell reminded her. 'Where's the second one, and who owns it?'

Esther nodded towards where Jack was standing with his mother Constance. 'You see that lady in the green hat who's talking to your new employer?'

'Yes.'

'That's his mother, and my mother-in-law. I plucked up the courage to tell her that her lawns are a disgrace, and she'll also be paying Billy a shilling a week.'

'So that's two shillings,' Nell replied thoughtfully, 'but that's hardly enough for a weekly wage, is it?'

Esther chuckled. 'When you have a chance to look round Barking, you'll see lots of lawns, many of which resemble jungles. Once the proud householders along our street see how neat our own lawns look, they'll be queuing up for his services.'

'And you'll be paying him a shilling yourself?'

'Of course, so that's three shillings. Now serve this man all the cakes he can get away with buying — the lady with her purse open is his wife and she'll be paying.'

Percy and Beattie had reached the cake stall and it had been some time since Esther had seen such a broad smile on Percy's face. She walked to the front of the sales position, leading Nell by the sleeve of her gown.

'Please be generous, Uncle Percy, and while you're at it, meet our new housemaid. Her name's Nell, and she's from the orphanage that I'm selling all these cakes for. The young man who'll be giving Aunt Beattie her change is also from the orphanage. His name's "Billy" and he's looking for work tending lawns in Barking.'

'So you're giving two orphans a start in life?' Percy beamed back.

'I suppose I am,' Esther agreed, 'although Billy may need a bit more of a helping hand.'

Percy smiled at Billy. 'Maintaining lawns, wasn't it?' he enquired. Billy nodded, and Percy turned to Beattie. 'One of those jam sponges for tea tonight, two cream buns for me, and whatever else you fancy. Just excuse me a moment.'

As he strode purposefully away from the stall, Jack came back with his mother in tow, and Constance looked enquiringly at Esther. 'I've rarely seen Percy move so fast. What's got into him?'

'No idea,' Esther beamed with self-satisfaction, 'but I'd like you to meet Nell, who'll be working as our housemaid once she leaves the orphanage. The young man with her is Billy, and he'll be scything your lawns.'

'And not before time, as you took the trouble to point out to me,' Constance replied to Esther before engaging Billy with a stern gaze. 'Make sure that you rake up the cut grass when you've finished and place it on my compost heap.

'Yes, Ma'am,' Billy assured her with a self-conscious grin as Beattie finished her purchases and he applied his mind to giving her the correct change.

Esther looked behind her when the hairs stood up on the back of her neck, and there — only a few feet away — stood someone she had been worrying about for weeks. 'Margaret!' she exclaimed with joyful surprise. 'Don't just hang back there — come and celebrate what a wonderful sales team we put together! But they're already spoken for, I'm afraid, since Nell will be living in as a domestic in our house, while Billy will be scything as many Barking lawns as he can find.'

'I hope you'll find it in your heart to forgive what I did,' Margaret said through what looked like tears of relief. 'You're being so lovely and generous, but I did a terrible thing, working in association with that awful woman who was killing babies. I really meant well, honestly I did.'

A tear formed in Esther's eye as she walked up to Margaret and gave her a big hug. 'Thanks to you, a considerable number of children like Nell and Billy here finished up being fed, clothed and educated. I can't speak for all of them, of course, but you can be proud of the work you do at the Holy Heart. It's not your fault if the woman who supplied you with those infants also took the lives of others — that had nothing to do with you and you haven't stopped qualifying for a good seat in Heaven just because you once knew the woman. You might with equal justification condemn her fishmonger.'

Margaret spluttered with laughter, then leaned forward and kissed Esther on the cheek. 'The best seat in Heaven will be reserved for you, Esther Enright. You're such a beautiful person. How's the baby coming along?'

'If it's a girl, it's going to be chorus girl, to judge by the high kicks,' Esther grimaced, 'now come and take your pick of the cakes that are left. My treat.'

A little over two hours later the stall was completely empty and the orphanage was just under ten pounds richer. Esther sat in a deckchair that the vicar had insisted on placing at her disposal, her feet up on a low stool, and Jack was assisting Billy to take down the stall itself, while Nell was carefully folding up the cloths that had covered it and chatting away happily to Margaret Meacher about her new job.

Jack looked up with a smile and nodded towards the gate. 'I don't know where he's been all this while, but here's Uncle Percy back to join us, and he looks like a beast of burden.'

'You owe the lady on the lemonade stall one and threepence,' he advised Beattie as he handed out the bottles. He'd bought one each for Nell and Billy, and as he handed Billy his he reached into his jacket pocket and took out a single sheet torn from his notebook.

'There you go, young man,' he said as he handed it to Billy. 'The names and addresses of four more customers. You'll now be earning another four shillings a week.'

'Where did you get those, Uncle Percy?' Esther asked with a broad smile from where she was seated.

Percy reached into the paper bag that Beattie was holding, extracted a cream bun and bit into it with a contented smile, making his audience wait until he'd swallowed the first mouthful before replying. 'It didn't take long for me to walk down Church Street and select a few overgrown gardens whose owners were advised that the local council had authorised me to issue formal warnings to those whose lawns were in need of a haircut, ahead of fining them if nothing was done to remedy the situation. I also advised them that an authorised lawn mechanic would be calling on them in the near future. It's my way of ensuring that at least one orphan doesn't fall by the wayside, after the horror stories I've been listening to lately.'

'Does that mean you're not resigning?' Jack asked eagerly.

Percy wagged a finger at him. 'There you go again, Jack Enright, jumping to conclusions. It's a very difficult decision to make, and one that will require at least one more cream bun.'

A NOTE TO THE READER

Dear Reader,

No apologies for involving the Enrights in an investigation of one of the greatest scandals of late Victorian England — one that was obvious to anyone with the lightest of social consciences but was never talked about.

Contraception was in its infancy then, but sex hadn't changed over the years. It was more common without the formality of wedlock, and in the poorer parts of London it was readily for sale. The consequences often took the form of inconvenient tiny helpless bundles, and there were predators waiting to make a living from them.

The mothers might sometimes be street prostitutes with no other way of surviving than to sell their bodies, or they might be 'nice' girls who'd been seduced by 'rotters', who either turned out to be already married, or who did a runner once the girl had missed a period or two. Another category of woman with an unwanted mouth to feed might be a respectable happily married woman whose husband's income, if it existed at all, simply couldn't run to a seventh or eighth addition to a family living in a squalid single room ten feet square.

The term 'baby farmers' was coined at around this time to describe people — usually, but not always, women — who advertised their willingness to 'adopt' unwanted babies for a suspiciously small fee. To salve the conscience of the mother, they would often pretend to be genuinely seeking a child of their own, or they might claim to be running a private orphanage out of the goodness of their hearts. Some didn't even bother with the pretence, and a few shillings handed over furtively in a darkened doorway along with a whimpering vulnerable bundle would mark the fate of the child that neither party had any illusions about.

We will never know how many helpless infants finished up strangled, starved, or stabbed through the heart with a hatpin, because the appalling infant mortality figures for England in the last decade of the Nineteenth Century were calculated by the number per thousand of the population, and the details of cause of death were vague to non-existent. Those who survived as orphans were little better off, and Dickens was not exaggerating.

I didn't set out to write a horror story, because I didn't need to. All I had to do was to give Jack and Percy Enright the task of investigating the events behind the discovery of several infant corpses against the background of what was really going on during that period, and the story wrote itself. I didn't invent Amelia Dyer, who may well have held the record for the number of infant murders committed by one person, but she certainly wasn't unique.

Women like the Harriet Crouch and Amy Jackson of this novel may be fictitious on one level, but they accurately reflect the revulsion that some people 'in the know' experienced regarding what was actually going on in the squalid orphanages while Queen Victoria was commissioning family photographs on the lawns of Osborne House. It's the job of an historical novelist to place the reader as accurately as possible back in the chosen ambience, and late Victorian London is better read about than experienced first-hand.

If you enjoyed this novel, it almost certainly wasn't for the warm glow that it engendered. But if so, my grateful thanks for letting me open some confronting doors. As ever, I would be delighted if you could post a review up on **Amazon** or **Goodreads**. Or, of course, you can try the more personal approach on my website, and my Facebook page: **DavidFieldAuthor**.

Happy reading!

David

davidfieldauthor.com

Sapere Books is an exciting new publisher of brilliant fiction and popular history.

To find out more about our latest releases and our monthly bargain books visit our website:
saperebooks.com

37350116R00111

Printed in Great Britain
by Amazon